An Arranged Marriage For A Lady

THE DARROW SISTERS
BOOK FOUR

FIONA MIERS

Chapter One

The morning sun filtered through the tall windows of the Weston townhouse, casting a warm, golden light across the drawing room. Eleanor had arranged elaborate vases of roses and lilies along the mantel, and the air was sweet with their scent. The soft rustle of silk, the affectionate hum of murmured conversation and laughter filled the air. Caroline sat poised on the edge of her seat, a glass of champagne in hand, delicate bubbles tickling her throat as she swallowed.

The warm-hearted chatter of her family surrounded her, a comforting symphony she had known all her life. A cascade of colourful ribbons and wrapping paper lay scattered at her feet, remnants of the birthday gifts she had just unwrapped.

"Oh, Eleanor, it's simply beautiful." Caroline held up a delicate bracelet that gleamed in the sunlight. The intricate gold links, set with sapphires and diamonds, were cool against her skin. She turned it over, admiring how it caught the light, and a rush of affection for her eldest sister welled in her chest. "You have spoiled me, and I love it."

Eleanor beamed from her place by the window, her hand resting gently on her growing belly. "I thought it suited you perfectly. Something to wear during the season—when you aren't galloping through the countryside."

Caroline laughed. "I haven't been on a decent ride since we arrived. But now that Silverthorne is here, I will probably visit Richmond Park, Wimbledon Common, and Hampstead Heath several times. I'll need that to stay sane during the season."

"What's wrong with Hyde Park, darling?" Caroline's mother, the dowager countess, furrowed her brow and stopped cooing over one of Olivia's twins to ask the question. Caroline's heart tightened at the sight of her mother's frown. No doubt, her love for Silverthorne was about to be questioned.

Olivia answered before Caroline could, "Rotten Row is too popular. Unless you get there at dawn, it's filled with riders and carriages, people intent on socialising rather than riding. The space is designed for being seen, not serious riding."

Caroline was quick to follow up. "Even at dawn, it's impossible to give Silverthorne her head—"

"You spoil that horse, Caroline." Alexander's deep voice cut through the chatter as he joined them, stopping only to kiss Eleanor's forehead gently. His presence always filled the room with authority, a weight that Caroline had grown used to but still bristled against. "In London, she walks sedately, or I will send her home."

Caroline clutched her new bracelet. Her tone was a little sharper than she intended. "I love her, and I love riding, Alexander."

"I am aware." At a glower from Eleanor, he let out a long sigh as he rubbed the back of his neck. "If you are accompanied by one of the men of the family and a groom, you may visit Richmond Park or Hampstead Heath for a slightly faster, longer ride."

Caroline picked at the seam of the sofa, her nails digging into the fabric. "Very well." She knew she sounded petulant but couldn't help it —it was her birthday. Her gaze shifted to her other sisters. Olivia gave her a wink, and Mary gave her an encouraging smile.

She had the best family ever, despite Alexander's heavy-handed instructions. Laughter bubbled up around her again, glasses clinked, and her brothers-in-law joined them, along with Alice and her fiancé, Lord Lynden. The warmth of the room, the closeness of her family helped make it the best birthday ever.

Alice sat beside her, smoothing her skirts. She gave her shoulder a playful nudge. "Have your thoughts turned to potential suitors?"

Caroline shook her head though a nervous flutter stirred in her stomach. "Honestly, Mary's experience has put me off a little. I'm excited, I guess." She traced the rim of her champagne glass absentmindedly. "But mostly, I just want to fall in love and be loved. I'm determined to do the same after watching you and my sisters marry for love."

Alice squeezed her hand, her grip warm and reassuring. "It will happen, darling. Hopefully, you don't have to suffer through too many balls, soirees, and dinners to meet him."

A knock sounded at the door, and Hawkins entered. "Lord Weston, may I have a word?"

It was unusual to hear the butler sound so tentative. But as Alice placed a large gift in her hand and Alexander left the room, the thought flew from her head.

It seemed like ages had passed before Alexander returned. His face was ashen, his usual composure shattered. He stood just inside the doorway, his eyes dark and shadowed. "Caroline, please, I will speak with you in my study."

His tone sent alarm bells ringing in her head. Something was wrong —very wrong. Her heart raced, and a heavy thudding sound echoed in her ribs. She stood quickly, her legs a little unsteady beneath her.

Eleanor stood as well, her voice tight and concerned. "What is it?"

Caroline blurted out. "I promise I won't go riding without—"

"It's not that Caroline." Alexander rubbed at his temple, and the weariness in his face made her heart sink further. "Eleanor, you may come as well if you wish."

"I do wish." Eleanor looped her arm through Caroline's and guided her to the door after Alexander.

Caroline didn't remember the walk to the study. Inside, the family lawyer, Mr. Harthing, stood with his hands clasped behind his back, staring out the window as if avoiding something unpleasant.

"Sit," Alexander said. "Let me pour you a sherry."

Caroline sank into the small leather sofa, her fingers trembling as she took the small glass he handed her. She stared at the amber liquid sloshing from side to side and felt her throat tighten. Whatever was going on couldn't be good.

"I do apologise for the intrusion, Lady Weston, Lady Darrow." Mr. Harthing bowed his head slightly. "I'm afraid an urgent matter has been brought to my attention. A letter arrived just this morning—"

"With news so urgent, you needed to interrupt Caroline's birthday celebration?" Eleanor wrapped her arm around Caroline's waist.

Caroline couldn't speak. Her heart pounded wildly as if trying to escape. She clutched Eleanor's arm, the anticipation almost unbearable.

Alexander waved a letter in the air, tension thickening with each passing second.

"Alexander, if you do not put us out of our misery this second," Eleanor stated with a scowl, "there will be consequences."

He folded and unfolded the official-looking parchment. "Mr. Harthing has brought to my attention a matter that concerns you, Caroline. A matter of your father's estate."

Caroline forced herself to sit up straighter, though every fibre of her being screamed at her to run. "The estate went to a distant cousin. There was little left for his wife and daughters. That's why we were so grateful when you took us all in after marrying Eleanor."

Alexander nodded, though his expression remained grim. "You know your father accrued considerable debt before passing, the largest of which he settled in the last weeks of his life."

Caroline frowned. "I'm not sure I understand. How does this concern me?"

Alexander hesitated, then looked directly into her eyes. "He settled the debt by contracting an agreement with the Marquis of Thornfield. You are to marry his second son, Lord Julian Osborn."

The words struck like a physical blow. Her breath caught as air rushed from her lungs. Married? To a man she had not even met? The room seemed to tilt, the walls closing around her. Blood drained from her face. She'd read about situations like this in her favourite novels. Her vision narrowed to a single point—the parchment in Alexander's hand, the letter that held her fate.

"What?" Her voice cracked, barely audible. She was standing on a cliff's edge, the ground crumbling beneath her feet.

Mr. Harthing cleared his throat. "As Lord Weston has summarised, the marriage was arranged to settle a serious debt. If it is not honoured, the marquess will likely pursue legal action. The consequences would be severe."

Severe? Caroline's stomach twisted painfully. She gripped the seat beneath her, her legs suddenly weak. "No." She shook her head as if denying the words would make them disappear. "This cannot be. I cannot marry a man I've never met."

"I will happily pay the debt myself." Alexander's face softened, but the pity in his eyes made her stomach sink even further. "But the marquess is resolute. He demands the contract be honoured. If we challenge him in court, it will be a public scandal, our family name dragged through the mud. Your reputation will be tarnished forever."

Tears of frustration welled in Caroline's eyes. She turned to Eleanor, her chest heaving with the weight of betrayal. "Father wouldn't do this to me. Is this a birthday joke?"

"No, darling, I'm sure it isn't." Eleanor rubbed small circles on Caroline's back. Even Eleanor's comforting touch did nothing to ease the knot of dread at her core.

Eleanor's tone sharpened. "Why is he so resolute? Caroline is lovely, but she is hardly a worthy payment for a sizeable debt."

Mr. Harthing gave an awkward cough before answering. "For two reasons, I believe, Lady Eleanor. First, the marquis is annoyed that he did not receive the expected payment. Second, his son has become a recluse since returning injured from the war. The marquis believes the young man will never find a wife on his own. The Darrow name is old, with descendants harking back to the thirteenth century, and forgive me, ladies, your beauty and cultured accomplishments are well known."

Caroline's mind reeled as her stomach churned. A recluse? The idea of being shackled to some war-scarred stranger, hidden away from society, filled her with icy terror.

Eleanor narrowed her gaze. "Surely, you can do something about this, Harthing?"

Eleanor's heartfelt plea broke the dam within Caroline's chest, and the first tear fell.

"Given the circumstances, winning a court case is a remote

possibility. But as Alexander has pointed out, it would come at a severe cost, even if we were to win. Our society is small, insular, and obsessed with reputation. A broken engagement would quickly become the subject of gossip, tarnishing you and your family. For women, social standing is fragile. Such gossip and its consequences can be particularly harsh and long-lasting."

It was nothing Caroline did not know. She desperately wanted Alexander to give her a way out, but he just shook his head. "I'm sorry, Caroline. There is no easy answer to this. We can try and fight the court case, but I fear you will still need to leave London, maybe even the United Kingdom, for some time."

"Perhaps it would help to consider it a matter of duty, Lady Caroline." Mr. Harthing's voice was filled with kindness. "You must understand that sometimes life offers us little choice. We must make the best of it."

Silence fell like an oppressive blanket. Alexander broke it. "It couldn't hurt to meet the man. You may find that you enjoy his company."

Caroline's chest tightened. *Duty.* The word tasted bitter on her tongue. She had spent her entire life dreaming of love and adventure, and now, with a single stroke of a pen, and her father's pen at that, her future had been decided without her consent.

"I cannot..." Her voice broke. "I cannot do this."

Eleanor pulled her into a tight hug, offering words of comfort, but it did little to soothe the storm brewing inside her. She barely registered the rest of the conversation, her thoughts spinning out of control. Marriage to a stranger. A debt she had no part in.

As the room began to blur around her, Caroline excused herself and fled to her bedroom. She needed to be alone to think.

But one truth remained—her future was no longer her own.

Chapter Two

Julian rode in silence, Brimstone's hooves clattering against the cobblestones. Each step jarred the old musket ball wound in his leg, sending sharp pulses of pain through the bone that had never fully healed. He grimaced but pressed on. The injury was a familiar ache, another reminder of battles fought and survived. At least he'd kept the leg... a small comfort.

His fingers tightened on the reins. Clenching harder didn't help, but he'd learned long ago to endure pain without complaint. The military had taught him that much.

London's streets blurred past, the usual din of the city drowned by his thoughts. Thornfield Townhouse loomed ahead, its stately façade glowing in the afternoon sun. He'd ridden to this door countless times, bracing for whatever command awaited in his father's suffocating study. Duty, obligation, and the crushing weight of expectations—it was always the same.

This time, the stakes were higher. His father's summons had been clear. It was time to wed and secure the family's legacy. Julian had no taste for the social games of the season, but resistance wasn't an option. The future of their name might depend on him, on his ability to produce an heir. A safety net should Robert fail. Not that Robert ever failed.

He guided Brimstone to the stables and dismounted. Pain flared up his leg, forcing him to grip the saddle for a moment. A stable hand approached, hesitantly. Julian didn't recognise him.

"Shall I take him, sir?"

Brimstone snorted, stomping a hoof in irritation. Julian murmured a calming word, running a hand down the dark bay's neck. The Friesian cross had been his steadfast companion through the war. Strong, disciplined, and dependable, the horse mirrored Julian himself.

"Where is Sam?" Julian kept a tight hold on the reins. Brimstone disliked meeting new people as much as he did.

"Here, sir." The young groom came running from the back of the stables. "I'll take him. We're old mates, aren't we, Brimmy? Come on, then."

The horse nickered in approval, letting Sam lead him away. Julian called his thanks and limped toward the back entrance. His father would prefer him to stride through the front doors like a true Thornfield heir, but Julian refused to parade his weakness. Better the servants' route.

Inside, his father waited in the study, seated behind the expansive desk like a throne. Tension thickened the still air. Julian settled into the leather armchair across from him, the weight of his father's intense stare beating against his head. A glass of brandy slid across the desk.

"You have not yet chosen a woman to wed." His father's voice was clipped, formal. Nothing unusual there.

Julian inclined his head. He had learned long ago not to show emotion during these conversations. "Is that why you summoned me to town?"

The marquess handed over a document. "You will marry Lady Caroline Darrow. The arrangements are finalised."

Julian's fingers tightened around the parchment. "A marriage contract?"

"Her father owed us a debt. This will settle it. Had you found a wife yourself, I might have considered other options. But you are thirty, Julian. It is time to fulfil your responsibilities. The family is sound. She has good connections and an adequate dowry. More than adequate, Weston has been unusually generous."

"And if I refuse?" The question came sharper than intended.

His father didn't flinch. He slid another document forward—a deed. "Refuse, and your estate remains mine. Agree, and it will transfer to you upon the marriage. Six months, Julian. That is all the time you have."

Julian's throat tightened. The estate—his sanctuary. The one place where he felt truly at peace, where battle scars felt less raw. His father was holding it hostage, and Julian knew he would not win if he fought this. He nodded stiffly. "When will you make the announcement?"

"After you meet her. She will attend the Carlisle ball in three days."

"And I am to attend."

"You know I can't stand sarcasm." The marquess narrowed his eyes. "You will charm her. Ensure she understands her place."

Julian rose, his father's words echoing in his ears. Duty. Honour. Sacrifice. He'd heard it all before. This marriage would be just another burden to carry.

He left the study, a flicker of unease creeping into his mind. Marriage! The war had taken too much from him and hardened him in ways that made such a notion impossible. He stiffened his shoulders. His estate was at risk. He would marry Lady Caroline Darrow and continue with his life.

Upstairs, he found Finch, his now ever-cheerful valet, waiting with a grin.

"Back from the lion's den, I see." Finch gave a slight bow. "How's the marquess? Still barking orders like a sergeant-major?"

Julian arched an eyebrow, though a faint smile tugged at his lips. "As commanding as ever, Finch."

"That's the spirit, sir. Nod, look thoughtful, it will keep the peace and save you trouble."

Julian shrugged out of his coat. "I'm glad to be out of his dusty travelling jacket. Sound advice, as always. But even your wisdom won't fix this."

Finch slid the coat from Julian's arms. "More duties, sir? You'll carry the day."

"Thanks for the confidence." Julian snorted as he turned, lifting his arms to let Finch unbutton his waistcoat. "Something like that."

Finch paused mid-button, giving him a sidelong glance. "What could ruffle your feathers this much?" He tapped his chin in exaggerated thought before his eyes lit up. "It wouldn't happen to be a lady, would it?"

Julian froze for a moment, the knot in his chest tightening. Finch was annoyingly perceptive at times. "You could say that."

Finch's grin widened, his voice dropping to a conspiratorial whisper. "Aha! So, you've finally been struck down by Cupid's arrow. It's about time, too, sir, if you don't mind me saying. I was beginning to think you'd wait until you were grey and creaky, picking out a lady with a magnifying glass like you were inspecting battle maps."

Julian shot him a dry look, though a hint of amusement flickered in his eyes. "Hardly Cupid's doing, Finch. A marriage arranged by my father. Lady Caroline Darrow."

Finch whistled low. "That's rich. The old man's gone and chosen your bride for you, has he? It saves you the trouble of courting, I suppose. Don't even need to dust off your charm."

"Charm isn't my strongest suit." Julian yanked off his cravat. "Nor is it necessary for a marriage of convenience."

"Convenience?" Finch scoffed. "Marriage is a battlefield all its own, where no matter what tactics you use, the lady always wins."

Julian laughed despite himself, sitting on the chair as Finch knelt to untie his boots. "If it's anything like the battlefield, I might be better prepared than most men."

Finch looked up, his eyes twinkling. "That you might, sir. But don't forget—on this battlefield, you're not fighting the French. You might be fighting a clever woman with more sense than any general we've ever known."

Julian grinned though unease churned beneath the surface. "I haven't even met her yet, Finch. I will do that at the Carlisle ball in a few days."

"And here I thought your days of danger were behind you."

Julian gave him a half-hearted glare. "It seems my father has no regard for my safety."

Finch tugged off the second boot with a grunt. "Well, sir, I reckon you'll survive the ball as you survived Waterloo. The trick is to avoid the dowagers. If you let 'em, they'll pin you in a corner quicker than a French bayonet."

Julian chuckled. "Noted. I'll keep my wits about me."

Finch stood and offered Julian a fresh shirt, his expression softening. "This Lady Caroline, what do you know of her?"

Julian sighed, slipping his arms into the shirt. "Good family, decent connections. Beyond that, I know nothing."

"I've heard worse reasons for a match, sir. Maybe she'll surprise you."

Julian stared into the distance, his jaw tightening. "Or maybe I'll find myself chained to someone who despises me as much as I despise this arrangement."

Finch shook his head with a sigh, moving to fasten the shirt buttons. "She could be as stubborn as a mule...or as sweet as treacle. Either way, you're stuck with her, so you might as well make the best of it."

Julian's lips pressed into a thin line as he stood. "Duty, Finch. It always comes down to duty."

Finch's expression softened again, his usual joviality giving way to something more sincere. "Aye, that it does, Colonel. But just because it's a duty doesn't mean you can't find a bit of joy in it, too. You've been through enough battles—you've earned it."

Julian forced a small smile in return. "Thank you, Finch. As always, I appreciate your... unique counsel."

Finch gave a mock bow and left Julian alone with his thoughts.

The estate—his sanctuary—was within reach, yet the path to securing it felt far more treacherous than any battlefield he'd ever crossed.

What of Lady Caroline? His father spoke as though her agreement were inevitable, as though she would bow neatly to the circumstances thrust upon her. But people did not yield so easily. Julian had seen enough of the world to know that.

Would she accept the arrangement without resistance? Or would she challenge it, refuse it, or demand something from him in return? He clenched his jaw, a flicker of unease twisting into something sharper. If she outright rejected the match, where would that leave him? Would he have to return the property to his father if he couldn't charm her into compliance?

Julian shook his head as he made his way toward his sitting room. He'd faced enemy fire, endured sleepless nights in the cold trenches, and navigated the razor's edge of life and death. So why did the prospect of convincing a woman to agree to an arranged marriage unsettle him so much?

He had three days to prepare for the Carlisle ball and whatever battle awaited him.

For the first time in years, Julian wasn't sure he had the strategy to win.

Chapter Three

The lively chatter of shopkeepers and the rustle of silk and delicate muslin gowns echoed off the narrow walls of the bustling laneway. The faint scent of lavender from sachets hanging in a nearby dressmaker's window drifted by. Caroline adjusted her grip on the small bundle of fabric samples in her arms, the delicate materials slipping slightly against her gloves.

Her cousin, Alice, strode ahead with determined cheer, the upcoming wedding casting a warm glow over every movement. A footman followed, his arms laden with bolts of lace and satin.

"Honestly, Caroline, you must at least pretend to care." Alice held up a shimmering length of ivory silk. The fabric seemed to catch the pale morning sunlight, glowing as though imbued with Alice's infectious excitement. "This is your future we're discussing."

Caroline gave the bolt of silk a cursory glance, her brow knitting. "Your future, Alice. Not mine." Her voice came out sharper than intended, but the words stuck in her throat like a bitter stone.

Alice's smile faltered for a fraction of a second before she smoothed it over, a determined brightness returning to her eyes. "You'll feel differently once you meet your reclusive lord. I hear he was quite handsome before he went off to war."

The words stung, though Caroline wasn't sure why. She wasn't the kind of shallow person who gave more credence to looks than character, was she? She let out a soft huff, adjusting the weight of the samples in her arms as though they were somehow to blame for her unease. "Once handsome or not, it hardly matters," she replied, her tone clipped. "This entire arrangement is monstrous."

Alice turned, nudging Caroline playfully with her elbow as they continued toward the dressmaker's shop. "Oh, don't be so dramatic. It could be worse—you could be marrying someone ghastly, or an old scoundrel, or a penniless curate, or a monster living in a ruin of a castle."

Caroline couldn't help laughing along. "Alright, I agree. Matters could potentially be worse." Her smile drooped, and her mouth pressed into a thin line when Alice turned away from her. She could also be marrying someone of her choosing. But the words remained locked inside her, heavy and unspoken.

Alice held up another bolt of fabric, a pretty and delicate lavender with intricate embroidery. "What do you think of this for the bridesmaids?"

Caroline glanced at the fabric. It was lovely, but its soft hue did little to soothe the knot of anxiety taking root in her chest. The colour reminded her of the ball gown, no doubt already spread across her bed, ready for her to attend Carlisle's grand affair.

"It's perfect," Caroline replied absently. Her thoughts were now firmly on the ball and the moment she would meet her betrothed—a man she had neither chosen nor wanted.

Alice went to find the shopkeeper to finalise her purchases, leaving Caroline with one of the footmen, and her thoughts spiralling in her head. What did she even know about this man except that he was the second son of the Marquis of Thornfield, a scarred war hero and recluse. Alex had told her he was taller than most men and walked with a noticeable limp. She'd probably notice him quickly enough, even at the ball, which would undoubtedly be a massive crush. That was, unless she hid herself away beforehand, an idea that blossomed in her head.

Alice announced the end of their shopping expedition and called for the carriage to be brought to the entrance to the laneway. "I'm sure Lady Beatrice has finished meeting her friends for coffee."

Caroline just nodded, her steps heavier with each passing moment.

Alice nudged her elbow. "Don't let Lady Beatrice see you with such a scowl. You will get a lecture on appropriate behaviour for young ladies.

Caroline took Alice's arm. "I'm sorry, I've ruined your shopping trip."

"Don't worry, I don't think anything could ruin my mood. And am hoping against hope that your betrothed is a jewel of a man beneath a rough exterior."

Caroline just wanted it all to go away,

Alice chatted about her wedding plans, her voice a comforting background hum, but Caroline barely registered the words. The thought of meeting and marrying Lord Julian filled her with dread, a dark weight pressing against her ribs. She clenched her hands tighter until her nails pressed painfully into her palms.

Caroline reached the waiting carriage and heaved a weary sigh while waiting for the footman to help her. The door swung open, and Lady Beatrice, impeccably poised as ever, peered out with one raised eyebrow, her cane resting lightly against her lap.

"Ah, there you are," Lady Beatrice perched small glasses on her nose. "I was beginning to think you'd been abducted by that dreadful haberdasher with the overly shiny buttons."

The footman handed Caroline into the carriage and stowed parcels and a bundle of samples next to her. She absentmindedly picked up the samples and crunched the fabric in her hands. "Sadly, no. I'm starting to think such a fate would be preferable to wedding shopping with Alice."

Lady Beatrice's lips curved into a faint smirk. "You look like a mule laden for the market, my dear. Are you planning to upholster an entire room, or is this some new and particularly gaudy fashion statement?"

"Alice insists that every ribbon and ruffle must be perfect for her wedding. I've been dragged along for the spectacle."

"Spectacle, indeed." Lady Beatrice tapped her cane lightly against the floor. "Weddings are nothing more than theatrical productions disguised as solemn occasions. You sit in a drafty church, endure interminable vows, and everyone pretends to enjoy the cake while gossiping about the bride's dress."

Caroline couldn't help but laugh, a small bubble of mirth breaking through her gloom. "What gossip would you spread about my wedding, Lady Beatrice?"

Lady Beatrice's eyes twinkled with mischief. "Well, that depends. Will you be walking down the aisle with a smile, or will we need to carry you kicking and screaming?"

"Neither," Caroline replied tartly. "I shall be the picture of decorum. You may want to keep smelling salts on hand in case I swoon from sheer misery."

Lady Beatrice tilted her head thoughtfully. "A wise precaution. However, I find swooning highly overrated. If one must make a scene, fainting is rather cliché. Far better to throw the bouquet directly at the groom and make your feelings known."

Caroline laughed again, the sound tinged with genuine amusement despite the weight in her chest. "I'll keep that in mind."

Lady Beatrice leaned forward slightly, her voice softening. "Now, my dear, don't forget—whether you march, swoon, or throw flowers, you'll marry into duty. But that doesn't mean you have to lose yourself in the process. If this Lord Osborne is half as disagreeable as his father, make it your mission to outwit him at every turn. Men are far more tolerable when they're confused. And if he is more like his dear mother, you may like the man."

Caroline's smile lingered as the carriage jolted, and Lady Beatrice settled back against the seat with a satisfied air. For the first time that day, the weight on her chest felt a fraction lighter. Even if her future was uncertain, she knew she could count on her family for support and to arm her with wit—and perhaps a few smelling salts—for whatever lay ahead.

Alice climbed into the carriage next to Lady Beatrice after ensuring her packages were secured to her liking, her grin undiminished. Caroline leaned back and let Alice and Lady Beatrice discuss the wedding with much laughing from Alice and almost as much tutting from Lady Beatrice.

As they approached the townhouse, chatter faded into silence, and Caroline's gloom returned. The shadow of her impending marriage loomed large, and no amount of lace or satin could lighten it.

The grand ballroom of Lady Carlisle's estate was a glittering masterpiece, its gilded walls and high ceilings aglow with the light of countless candles. Crystal chandeliers hung like celestial constellations, shimmering reflections on the polished marble floor. Music swirled through the room, blending with the hum of laughter and conversation. Yet, for all its opulence, Caroline felt like a thread pulled taut, her heart racing as though it might snap.

She stood near the refreshment table, her fingers delicately wrapped around the stem of her glass. Outwardly poised, she was inwardly waging war against the tension knotting her stomach. Her pale lilac muslin gown fell in soft folds, and her golden hair was swept into an elegant knot adorned with a jewelled comb and ostrich feathers dyed to match. However, none of those preparations gave her comfort.

Even without Eleanor's help, she spotted Lord Julian Osborne when he entered the room.

So this was the man her father wanted her to marry.

He moved through the room with undisguised reluctance, his dark hair neatly combed back, his broad shoulders filling out the severe lines of his evening coat. He carried himself with the quiet confidence of a man who had seen far too much. His expression—an unreadable mix of indifference and irritation—heightened her unease, and she gave up trying to fight the knot of tension in her stomach.

He was, she conceded reluctantly, still a very handsome man. He could have worn his military uniform, with numerous medals pinned to his chest, turning heads wherever he went. Instead, he'd chosen the subdued elegance of civilian eveningwear. What did his choice mean about his attitude regarding war? Was it humility? A desire to move beyond war? Or indifference to the trappings of glory. The slight limp did not detract from his commanding presence. If anything, it added an air of gravitas, as did the faint scar slashed across his brow.

It was not long before he spotted Alexander and made his way toward them, his movements measured, his face set. She swallowed hard, straightened her shoulders, and pasted a polite smile on her lips. She had no choice but to meet him. Eleanor and Alexander stood next to her, waiting to introduce him. Besides, what was the point of hiding away? She had promised Alexander that she would at least meet the man.

Alexander stepped closer, his usual calm air giving her some much-needed reassurance. He offered her a faint smile as he gestured toward the man who stopped before her. "Caroline, may I present Lord Julian Osborne, the younger son of the Marquess of Thornfield." He turned to Julian. "Osborne, this is my sister-in-law, Lady Caroline Darrow, youngest daughter to the Earl of Grantham."

He did not need to mention her place within the hierarchy, but Caroline was glad he did. Julian might outrank her as the son of a marquis, but not by much, and they socialised within the same circles.

"Lady Caroline." He bowed, his deep, smooth voice utterly devoid of warmth. "It is a pleasure to meet you."

Caroline suppressed the sharp retort that sprang to her lips. *Is it?* Instead, she dipped into a flawless curtsy. "Lord Osborne, the pleasure is mine."

Rising, she met his steady, appraising gaze head-on. His steel-grey, sharp eyes held hers for a fraction longer than was strictly polite. The air between them seemed to crackle.

Lord Julian spoke first. "I trust you are enjoying the ball?" His tone suggested he cared little for her answer.

"Indeed." Her cheerful tone had an edge sharp enough to cut glass. "There is nothing quite so delightful as being introduced to a stranger one is expected to marry."

Alexander coughed into his hand, clearly wishing he had avoided this task, but Julian's lips quirked ever so slightly. "I take it you find the arrangement disagreeable."

Caroline tilted her head, her smile never wavering. "Do you not?"

"I have long since accepted that life is filled with duties." Caroline's jaw stiffened. How could he be so maddeningly calm? "This is another of them."

She let out a soft laugh, though there was steel beneath it. "How fortunate for you, my lord, that you are adept at fulfilling duties. I fear I may not be quite so practised."

His gaze lingered on her, trying to decide whether she was mocking him outright. "Perhaps practice will come in time, Lady Caroline."

"Or perhaps," she said sweetly, "I will find a way to keep life interesting despite its duties."

For the first time, his composure seemed to waver. His lips pressed into a thin line, though his eyes held a flicker of something that might have been amusement—or irritation. "Interesting can be unpredictable."

She raised an eyebrow, her smile widening. "Exactly."

Alexander cleared his throat. If he were disturbed by their exchange, he wouldn't have shown it. "Osborne, perhaps you would escort Caroline to the dance floor? I believe the next set is a waltz."

Julian hesitated for a fraction of a second before offering his arm. "If the lady is amenable."

Caroline took his arm with practised grace, her gloved hand resting lightly on his sleeve. "I would be delighted, my lord."

They glided to the dance floor, the weight of countless sharp gazes targeting her back. The soft rustle of her gown and the rhythmic click of Julian's polished boots on the marble seemed deafening even in the noisy hum. Her heart pounded in her chest, a wild, relentless rhythm that belied the calm, composed expression she forced onto her face.

She met Julian's gaze briefly, and an unfamiliar heat crept up her neck. Something hidden within his eyes stirred her curiosity. What had made him a grumpy recluse? From everything she'd heard, he'd been the typical second son around town before joining the military. Something about him flickered just out of reach, drawing her in despite the promise she made to herself to stay detached.

They took their places, and she couldn't stop herself from teasing him. "I hope you are an accomplished dancer, my lord."

He lifted his brow but didn't respond, extending his hand, palm steady, and waiting for hers.

She hesitated, a strange fluttering low in her stomach. A single dance had never felt so loaded in meaning.

Her gloves whispered against her skirts as she raised her hand and placed it lightly in his. Perhaps it was just her imagination, but somehow, his warmth bled through the thin layers of fabric as though their kid gloves were no barrier at all. Her pulse quickened. His hand was so much larger than hers, his grip firm but not unkind. She had to remind herself to breathe.

She shouldn't have teased him. Her conscience prickled. His limp, though slight, was evidence of a wound that must have pained him far more than she could imagine. She pushed the thought aside, determined to keep her footing in this strange, unspoken battle. After all, hadn't Lady Beatrice told her all was fair in love and war? It also had to apply to arranged marriages, probably mainly to arranged marriages. "I would hate to find myself caught in yet another of your duties performed adequately."

His lips twitched, and the faintest flicker of amusement ghosted across his face. "I assure you, Lady Caroline, I am more than adequate."

Her heart gave a peculiar lurch at the quiet confidence in his words. She arched a brow, meeting his gaze with a sparkle in her eye. "I suppose we shall see."

As the music began, Julian led Caroline into the waltz with practised precision. His movements were smooth and controlled despite his limp and surprisingly graceful for a man who seemed so rigid. Caroline allowed herself to relax as the music swirled around them. She had to admit his presence was undeniable. His height, straight-backed posture, and guarded expression called out his station in life.

Her free hand rested lightly on his shoulder. Strength seemed to radiate beneath the fine fabric of his evening coat, something she had never noticed in any of her other dancing partners. Had she just never noticed, or was this man different? The closeness of their bodies sent a fresh wave of awareness coursing through her, and she had to focus on keeping her steps in time with his.

She needed this dance to end. She had to retreat and create some distance from the strange, disarming feeling that his nearness evoked. But she couldn't run off the dance floor like some inexperienced debutante, though that expression was apt. The music held them together, and Julian's steady presence anchored her as they moved in perfect synchrony across the floor.

Caroline's cheerful mask never faltered, but thoughts and questions whirled through her mind. Who was this man? She had expected to find him boringly insufferable, but she found herself intrigued. Beneath his gruff exterior was a man she could not yet understand. A man she wasn't sure whether to fear, challenge, or maybe one day, trust.

The waltz ended, the final notes fading into a background hum of conversation.

Julian released her hand and stepped back, bowing slightly. She curtsied in return, her heart still racing like she had been running rather than dancing.

"Thank you, Lady Caroline." His words had no warmth, but his gaze lingered on her longer than necessary, leaving her breathless.

"The pleasure was mine, Lord Osborne." Her voice stayed steady despite the flutter in her chest.

"Good evening." He didn't wait for her answer, he just turned and walked away. The space where his hand had rested felt strangely cold, and she curled her fingers into her palm to capture the fading warmth.

Eleanor crowded her shoulder. "Well?"

"He is not quite like I expected. And yet, I can't decide whether that is a comfort or a danger."

Eleanor pressed a glass of champagne into her hand. He disappeared into the crowd, and Caroline tightened her fingers around the stem. He was insufferable—cool, detached, and maddeningly sure of himself. And yet, as much as she hated to admit it, the exchange left her strangely exhilarated. Her heart still raced as she replayed their words in her mind.

If he thought Caroline would be docile in this arrangement—she targeted his back with a wry smile—then he knew nothing about her at all.

Chapter Four

Julian stood near an upstairs window, one hand behind his back, the other gripping his walking cane, his expression neutral. Outside, a carriage rolled to a halt, its polished exterior glinting in the late afternoon light. The footman opened the carriage door, and one by one, the Westons stepped out. Finally, she emerged—Lady Caroline Darrow.

His composure wavered. He huffed to himself. Where was the self-control he prided himself upon when he needed it? He hadn't expected to feel such a pull toward the woman his father chose for him, yet here he stood, concealed in the shadows like an untried schoolboy, newly emerged into society and nursing an unseemly infatuation with his first glimpse of beauty.

And a beauty she was. The afternoon sunlight caught the golden undertones of her hair, and artful waves framed her delicate features. Her gown, a muted shade of blue trimmed with delicate lace, perfectly highlighted her vivacity.

It wasn't just her appearance that drew his attention. As they walked to the steps, Lady Weston said something that sent laughter spilling into the crisp air, a sound so warm and inviting, it felt out of place against the austere façade of Thornfield House. Lady Caroline's wide and genuine smile gave her a delicate radiance. He wanted to be the one to bring that sort of smile to her face.

It was unsettling.

She seemed to vibrate with life, every movement infused with a vitality that contrasted sharply with the quiet, measured existence he'd cultivated since returning from the war. She was like sunlight streaming into a room long accustomed to shadows. He was both drawn to and wary of her.

His jaw tightened as he paced to the top of the stairs. Damned leg. He'd no choice but to use the cane after his long ride to town, and he'd gone without the cane at Carlisle's ball two nights ago for the sake of appearances.

He had prepared himself for a simpering debutante, overly docile, eager to please, someone like his brother's wife, little more than the breeding mare she knew herself to be. Lady Caroline was none of those things. She was spirited, lively, and he suspected, entirely capable of making his life difficult.

She stepped into the house and her gaze flitted across the grand entrance hall, taking in the dark wood panelling, the marble floors, and the towering staircase. When her eyes landed on him, she paused briefly, her head tilted. Her polite smile remained, but the open curiosity in her expression caught him off guard. She was neither intimidated by his stature nor his history, nor was she dismissive of him as a cripple.

She was assessing him. Assessing him as a challenge or as an enemy?

Julian took the stairs one at a time, slower than he would have liked, but after long practice, he didn't have to watch his feet every step. He inclined his head in greeting, his face impassive, though his pulse quickened. "Lady Caroline, welcome to Thornfield House."

"Lord Osborne." She held his gaze. "Thank you for personally receiving us."

She curtsied with flawless grace, her movements effortlessly poised. It was the sort of polished greeting he had witnessed countless times, yet something about it struck him differently. Julian's chest tightened, a faint, unfamiliar unease settling there. The sharp intelligence glinting in her eyes unnerved him more than he cared to admit, a reminder that she was not some pliant debutante eager to please. She was assessing him as surely as he was assessing her, and the weight of her scrutiny left him momentarily off balance. She was not what he expected—and for a man who thrived on control and predictability, that was a profoundly unsettling realisation.

Julian swallowed his brandy and gazed at all the guests his father had invited to this damned dinner. Lord and Lady Weston laughed with one of his father's cronies. The Duke and Duchess of Wallingford spoke with his father. Lord and Lady Everhart seemed to be receiving a lecture from his brother, but that was normal for Robert, who liked to hear his own voice and express his opinions.

Lady Caroline was talking sweetly with his cousin, Isabella, and sister, Georgina. The three were the same age, though Isabella was soft and pliable, whereas Lady Caroline was anything but. Georgina had been spoilt all her life, and it showed. His Aunt Matilda, standing in as hostess, circled the room, engaging every guest with a warmth that reminded him of his dear mother.

He caught her eye, and she meandered to him. "Try to mix and mingle, please, Julian. And don't forget, you will be escorting Lady Caroline to dinner. Your places are marked on the table."

He gave her a stiff nod. He'd attended enough of these dinners to know that his father and aunt, as host and hostess, would occupy one end of the table each, the duke and duchess plus his brother and his wife close to the head of the table also. He would be somewhere in the middle as befitted his middling rank, and no doubt his aunt had placed Lady Caroline opposite him to allow for some interaction without breaking social decorum.

He couldn't wait for the night to end, yet he had to survive the dinner, port with the gentlemen, then the drawing room with the ladies, dancing, card games and the inevitable subtle flirtation after it.

They were called to dinner as he fought back his bad mood. He sat opposite Lady Caroline and between Isabella and Lady Everhart, Caroline's sister, Mary.

As Julian settled into his seat, he caught a flicker of movement from across the table. Lady Caroline was smoothing her napkin onto her lap with a delicacy that belied the sharp glint in her eye. Her gaze met his briefly before she turned to speak with her sister, Lady Mary, who was seated to his left. Despite himself, Julian's ears pricked as their conversation carried across the table.

"Mary, did you see the paddocks as we arrived?" Caroline asked, her voice lilting with genuine enthusiasm. "Thornfield's stables must be impressive, like the grounds."

Mary smiled, casting a sly glance toward Julian. "Oh, yes. I imagine they are. It's a pity we won't see them tonight, but perhaps Lord Osborne would be willing to give us a tour."

Julian raised an eyebrow, his tone dry as he responded. "Are you in the habit of visiting stables during dinner parties, Lady Mary?"

Mary's eyes sparkled with amusement. "Only when the stables are rumoured to house exceptional horses, my lord. And I've heard that Thornfield's are among the best."

Caroline leaned forward slightly, her tone bright and teasing. "Is that true, Lord Osborne? Or does the estate rely on reputation alone?"

Julian deliberately set his wine glass down, the weight of its base settling against the table with a muted thud. "The stables are not for show, Lady Caroline. The horses are bred for utility, not paraded as trophies."

The faintest smile curved her lips. Her eyes sparkled with a curiosity that Julian found both disarming and exasperating. "Utility, you say?" she repeated her voice light but her gaze sharp. "I suppose that means they wouldn't suit riders with a bit more… spirit?"

Julian blinked, caught off guard for just a fraction of a second. She had a way of twisting words, of pulling meaning from them that he hadn't intended but couldn't entirely refute. "Utility does not mean lack of spirit, Lady Caroline." He ignored the subtle sting of her challenge. "It means they serve a purpose beyond preening in the paddock."

"Ah, so they're disciplined. Reliable. Predictable." Caroline's smile widened, her tone carrying a hint of playful defiance.

"Precisely." Julian snapped. A flicker of unease grew in his chest. She wasn't teasing aimlessly, there was intent in her words, a thread he couldn't quite grasp.

"Predictable sounds dull." Her polite tone might have been genuine were it not for the glint in her eye. "Surely, you don't find all unpredictability objectionable, my lord."

Julian's jaw tightened as he resisted the urge to look away. Her words landed with more weight than he cared to admit, striking at truths he'd spent years trying to bury. He prided himself on control—of his life, emotions, and responsibilities. Had she seen through the calm façade he worked so hard to maintain?

"I find unpredictability is best tempered by a steady hand." His tone was more clipped than he meant, but it was too late to take it back now.

Her laugh was soft, musical, and entirely too self-assured. "And here I thought a spirited horse—or rider—might be better matched by one willing to rise to the challenge."

The room seemed to fade for a moment, the low hum of conversation and clink of cutlery melting into the background. There was only her for Julian—animated, luminous, and utterly fearless. She wasn't simply speaking about horses, she was talking about him, testing him.

Two could play at that game. "You seem very certain of your abilities, Lady Caroline. Perhaps you'd care to put them to the test?"

Her eyes narrowed slightly, though the smile never left her lips. "Are you offering me the chance to ride one of your 'utilitarian' mounts, my lord?"

Amusement spread through the guests near them, but Julian didn't flinch. "I am. Brimstone. He's served me well on the battlefield, though I wonder how he might respond to a rider as spirited as you, Lady Caroline."

Isabella, seated beside him, gasped softly. "Brimstone? Julian, you're not serious. He's barely manageable on his best days."

"Barely manageable war horse?" Caroline repeated, her expression brightening with what could only be exhilaration. "He sounds perfect."

Julian leaned back in his chair, studying her with renewed curiosity. Did she truly see life as an adventure to be seized, or was she refusing to back down from a challenge? Either way, he was both irritated and impressed.

"You may find him less perfect than you imagine. He requires a firm hand and steady nerves."

"Then we should get along splendidly," Caroline replied with a dazzling smile. "I'll take that as an invitation, Lord Osborne."

"It was." Julian couldn't suppress the faint tug of a smile. "But don't say I didn't warn you."

"I never heed warnings," she quipped, turning back to her sister Mary, who was barely suppressing a laugh. "Life's far more interesting that way."

The laughter rippling around the table at her remark carried an undercurrent of tension, as though everyone knew this battle of words might soon escalate into something far more compelling. Julian leaned back in his chair, allowing himself a rare moment of amusement. She was fiery, clever, and entirely too confident—but for the first time in a long while, he felt the flicker of something unexpected: anticipation.

Not that he could let her ride Brimstone, no matter how pretty her plea.

Chapter Five

Caroline sat at her writing desk, a cup of tea untouched beside her, staring absently at a blank page in her notebook. She waited for Eleanor to finish dressing so they could ride together before the social scene crowded Hyde Park. Usually, Caroline would have filled the page, jotting notes to friends or sketching a scene from her recent adventures. But today, her thoughts were a whirlwind. She'd already accidentally dropped two blobs of ink on the page.

The dinner at Thornfield House lingered in her mind. Every word and interaction with Lord Julian was on continual repeat. He had been as composed and taciturn as at the ball, yet interest flickered behind his sombre eyes. He kept a quiet sense of humour tightly reined.

She'd enjoyed their verbal sparring. No, not enjoyed. Was intrigued.

This unwanted attraction to him was merely a curiosity, and that was that.

After dinner, the gentlemen rejoined the ladies in the drawing room, and Julian surprised her with a tour of the Thornfield stables. She hadn't expected him to indulge her interest or show anything of his authentic self while doing so, but his calm composure slipped, and he showed genuine pride and affection when he spoke about his horses.

Brimstone was beautiful, his sleek coat gleaming like polished mahogany in the flickering lantern light. Battle-scarred like his rider but no less handsome for it. She hadn't even attempted to hold in a gasp when she first saw him. The dark bay Friesian cross stood tall in his stall —he had to be sixteen, maybe seventeen hands high. His well-balanced frame showed off powerful hindquarters, a deep chest, and a muscular neck that arched beautifully. His intelligent eyes watched her with the same quiet appraisal as Lord Julian.

She and Mary had listened open-mouthed when Julian explained Brimstone's service in the war and his temperament—steady under fire yet spirited enough to require a skilled rider. She'd met his challenge with a teasing smile and a tacit promise to prove herself capable. Brimstone had responded to her presence with a snort and a flick of his tail, quite unimpressed.

No matter, she would win him over.

"Perhaps he doesn't believe me." She patted Brimstone's powerful neck. "But I've never met a horse I can't make friends with."

Julian had replied with a single arched brow and a faint smile that disappeared almost as quickly as it had come. It was maddening how he could convey so much without saying a word.

He'd challenged her to ride Brimstone, which she had accepted. An offer he hadn't repeated in the stables. Perhaps he regretted it. No matter. She would call him a fraud instead of a gentleman if he tried to retract. She was a fine horsewoman, and now that she'd met Brimstone and heard his story, she wanted to ride him. Surprising his master with her skill would be a bonus.

Thornfield House had left her unsettled, but not in the way she dreaded. Julian was not cold or cruel, nor was his family unkind. But the darkness within him called to her in a way that made her feel like she was standing at the edge of a vast, uncharted ocean.

She rose from her desk and crossed the room to the window. A few carriages rattled in the street below, kicking up the remnants of last night's rain. She placed a hand against the cool glass, her reflection staring back at her, pensive and unsure.

What was it about Julian that unsettled her so? It wasn't just his reserved manner or how he seemed to weigh his words like a man choosing his weapons. The glimpses of something more profound—a soldier's discipline, a rider's humble mastery, a man's quiet loneliness—made her want to know more.

Caroline shook her head at her foolish thoughts. He was just a man chosen for her by circumstances over which she had no control.

Alexander had asked her to meet the man and give him a chance. She'd done that. If she begged Alexander to get her out of the arrangement, he would. But the thought of leaving her beloved sisters, maybe even the country, filled her with dread.

Besides, if she were being honest with herself—which she wasn't and had no plans to anytime soon—she'd have to admit that when she thought of Julian's sharp wit, the challenge in his eyes, and the warmth in his voice when he'd spoken of Brimstone, she couldn't help but want to find out more.

A knock sounded at her door, and her maid, Nell, admitted Eleanor.

"Are you ready? We want to miss the crowds, don't we?" Eleanor sailed into the room with one hand on her hip.

Caroline shook her head at her sister. "I am ready and have been waiting—"

"My goodness," Eleanor interrupted. Her expression brightened. "Your new habit is divine. The pale blue suits you perfectly, like fresh spring air. And the ornamentation! Even the military top brass wouldn't dare accuse you of borrowing their style—it's far too elegant."

Caroline smoothed the front of her jacket with a small smile. "You approve, then? I wasn't entirely sure about the braiding. It felt rather bold."

Eleanor arched an eyebrow. "It's positively brilliant. How the jacket defines the figure—at least half the men in the park will swoon into their stirrups. And that plume." She gestured toward the Glengarry cap in her hand. "A touch theatrical with those sweeping feathers, perhaps, but just the right amount. You could lead a cavalry charge and still look like the star of a salon."

Caroline laughed, adjusting the blue satin ribbon on her cap. "I think I'll leave cavalry charges to Lord Osborne."

"I hope we bump into him in the park. He told us he rode early every morning, and heavens only knows this is more than early. I hope he notices you." Eleanor's gaze sparkled with a teasing glint. "Men can be infuriatingly oblivious. They can ride alongside you and not register how splendid you look."

Caroline shook her head with mock exasperation. "I'm sure he'd notice if my sleeves weren't braided nearly halfway up the arm or my cravat wasn't tied into an adequate bow."

Eleanor chuckled. "You underestimate him, dearest. He may be brooding, but even brooding men have eyes. If nothing else, that glorious pale blue will catch his attention."

Eleanor's words gave Caroline pause. A small part of her hoped they would meet Julian and that he might take notice. She straightened the lace ruffles at her wrists and smoothed her gloves, quietly satisfied in knowing her habit was a showstopper.

Eleanor suddenly grabbed her hand and tugged her from the room. "I don't think this riding habit can be let out anymore." She patted her tiny tummy. "Did I tell you what the modiste told me?"

Eleanor continued before Caroline could answer that she had heard this story several times, "She was steadfast. Ladies in a delicate condition do not ride."

Caroline just laughed as they headed to the stables. Eleanor had already found a modiste who was happy to make her anything. Marriage may have calmed Eleanor, but she still had a wild streak that sometimes came out to play.

The crisp morning air filled Caroline's lungs as she urged Silverthorne on, the mare's powerful stride sending a thrill through her. The rhythmic drum of hooves against soft earth and the regular creaking of her saddle provided a welcome reprieve from the chaos of her thoughts. This was her sanctuary. Her space to breathe, think, and feel in control of her life, if only for a short while.

Behind her, Eleanor rode at a slower pace. Caroline glanced back to see her sister's shoulders swaying with weariness, her cheeks faintly flushed. "Why didn't you say you were tiring?"

"You're pushing me too hard, Caroline." Eleanor's breathless laugh softened the words. "I'm not quite as spry as you are these days."

Caroline slowed Silverthorne to a walk and turned back. "You should have stayed home and rested. You've been overdoing things."

"Nonsense." Eleanor brushed the concern aside with a wave of her hand, though her shoulders sagged with relief at the slower pace. "I refuse to miss out on a good ride. Besides, having a moment alone with you is rare these days. Alice's wedding preparations have overtaken everything."

Caroline smirked, guiding Silverthorne alongside Eleanor's horse. "She's relentless, isn't she? I've never seen anyone fuss so much over a table setting."

Eleanor chuckled. "Alice knows what she wants, and Lord Lynden now indulges her every whim. The two of them together are meticulous beyond reason."

"They'll have the most perfectly coordinated wedding in all of London." Caroline let out a breath of mock annoyance. "Though I overheard Alice debating whether lilies and roses are too provincial."

"The modiste will faint if she asks for more changes to her dress."

"I know. She's already changed it three times."

"She will certainly make a grand entrance." Eleanor shook her head. "She has a wreath of delicate lilies, crafted from lace and silk cord, adorning the lower edge of her slip, and the open robe and train are finished with lace flounces and a charming mix of lilies and roses."

Eleanor's expression softened. "Speaking of grand entrances, have you or Alice decided on your gowns yet?"

Caroline gave a dramatic sigh. "Alice has chosen lilac fabric that is so weighed down in lace that it may not be easy to walk in. If it pleases Alice, I'll endure it."

"At least you won't have to worry about your gown fitting on the day." Eleanor drifted her hand absently to her growing belly again. "I'm beginning to wonder if mine will even button."

Caroline's grin widened. "You'll look beautiful, buttons or not. And if it doesn't fit, we'll drape you in silk and call it the height of fashion."

Eleanor laughed, shaking her head. "I doubt Alice would agree. She might march me straight to the modiste for alterations."

"I wouldn't put it past her." Caroline reached over to squeeze Eleanor's gloved hand. "But truly, Eleanor, you'll outshine everyone there. That glow of yours isn't just from the ride."

Eleanor's cheeks pinkened, though she smiled warmly. "I'll take your word for it."

They fell into a companionable silence, the sounds of London fading as they ventured deeper into the park. Early morning light still filtered through the trees, casting long, soft shadows on the dew-dappled grass. The scent of damp earth and faint traces of lilac filled the air, and contentment filled Caroline's chest. For all the chaos of Alice's wedding and the looming uncertainties of her future, moments like this —riding with Eleanor, teasing and laughing—were a balm to her soul.

Eleanor whispered, "Lord Osborne approaches." And the peace shattered.

Caroline's gaze snapped to the imposing figure riding toward them on his tall, dark stallion. Her stomach knotted, though she hid it with a polite smile. Lord Osborne had a way of unsettling her—if not with his penetrating gaze or air of supreme control, he rattled her composure with just a few words.

"Lady Caroline, Lady Weston." He drew closer, inclining his head in a polite nod. His dark eyes met Caroline's, a hint of amusement in his expression.

"Lord Osborne." Caroline's voice was steady even as her pulse quickened. "What a surprise."

Julian's mouth almost formed a smile before settling back into neutrality. "I didn't realise Hyde Park was reserved for you alone."

Eleanor cleared her throat. "I see a bench. It's time for me to rest. I shall leave you two to your conversation." She called one of the grooms to follow her, leaving the eldest behind to provide a chaperone for Caroline.

Caroline shot her sister a look that promised retribution later, but Eleanor only smiled sweetly before urging her horse forward, the groom following dutifully. The groom stayed behind as a silent chaperone but far enough away to leave the two of them to their exchange.

Caroline shifted in her saddle, trying to ignore the growing tension in the air. "Shall we ride?"

Julian raised his brow. "Another challenge, Lady Caroline?"

"Perhaps." She tilted her chin, feigning nonchalance. She hadn't meant to challenge him on or to anything, just wanting to ride, but she wasn't one to back down. "Unless you fear I'll leave you behind."

They rode side by side, the park empty but for a few other serious equestrians. Caroline focused on the freedom of the experience—the wind in her hair, the rhythmic motion of Silverthorn beneath her. This is what it felt like to feel truly alive, the world stripped bare of expectation and judgment.

Caroline glanced at Julian, his expression as composed and unreadable as ever. Determined to break the tension, she leaned slightly toward him.

"Lord Osborne, if I recall correctly, you suggested at dinner that I would never manage Brimstone."

Julian's brow lifted slightly. "I recall stating it as fact."

"And yet here we are." She patted Silverthorne's neck. "I would like to see whether Brimstone is as difficult as you claim, or if his reputation is merely his rider's vanity."

Julian gave a soft huff, his lips curving into a faint smile. "You truly expect me to let you ride him?"

"Of course. You issued the challenge, I accepted, and I keep my word." She didn't need to add that she expected him to keep his word.

"He's not accustomed to other riders." Julian huffed softly. "I doubt he'll take kindly to being handled by anyone other than me."

Caroline raised an eyebrow. "Is this your way of backing out?"

Julian paused, his jaw tightening. "Not at all. I am, however, aware of the danger. Brimstone doesn't suffer fools."

"Fortunately, I am no fool," she quipped. "Besides, I came prepared." She called the groom to help her dismount and reached into her pocket. She pulled out several small pieces of carrot. "Your warhorse and I are already acquainted."

Julian's eyes widened slightly as she offered the carrot to Brimstone. The stallion pricked his ears forward, sniffing the treat before nuzzling her hand and taking it delicately.

Caroline smiled and stroked his neck with ease. "It seems Brimstone and I are already friends."

Julian frowned, though the faint amusement in his eyes betrayed him. "Very well. But don't blame me if he decides you're not to his liking mid ride."

She laughed. "Silverthorne isn't always well-behaved for other people. Have you brought your best game this morning?"

Caroline murmured to Brimstone and patted his neck. The groom assisted in swapping the saddles, giving a measured glance at Julian as if to silently question his judgment. "Are you certain, my lord? The stallion is a handful."

Julian merely nodded. "She insists. Let us see if Brimstone agrees."

Brimstone stood placidly throughout it all. Silverthorne showed her discontent until Caroline soothed her.

Finally, each saddle was girthed to the groom's satisfaction, and he helped swing her up, her riding habit draping elegantly as she adjusted her seat. Julian hovered nearby as if he expected the stallion to protest, but to his apparent surprise, Brimstone remained calm.

The groom stepped back, arms crossed, evidently reserving his judgement.

"He likes me." Caroline settled herself like she had been born to ride the imposing creature. "Shall we try a sedate canter?"

Julian gave an incredulous laugh. "Sedate? I doubt Brimstone knows the meaning of the word. Regardless, do not go faster than a canter."

Caroline clicked her tongue and urged the stallion forward. Brimstone moved leisurely, his powerful muscles rippling beneath her as though testing her resolve. She kept her posture steady, her grip firm but light. For a fleeting moment, she thought she had mastered him.

Then Brimstone surged ahead.

The stallion's powerful canter turned into a full gallop, the sudden acceleration sending a thrill through Caroline's chest. She leaned forward instinctively, her body moving with his as the wind whipped at her riding habit and tugged at the ribbons on her hat. Her pulse raced, but not with fear—this was exhilaration, pure and unrestrained.

Julian called out behind her, sharp and commanding, "Caroline!"

But she paid him no mind. This was her moment, her challenge to conquer. She adjusted her weight subtly in the saddle, guiding Brimstone with a delicate pull of the reins. The stallion responded, powerful and eager, his hooves pounding the soft earth in a rhythm that echoed the wild thrum of her heartbeat.

What a magnificent creature! Her laughter spilled as they raced forward. He wasn't just a horse, he was strength and freedom embodied. And she felt alive, as though the world had shrunken to this perfect moment where she and Brimstone were one.

The sound of pursuing hooves grew louder, and she glanced over her shoulder to see Julian astride Silverthorne—his whole posture exuding anger—and the groom not far behind him. She couldn't dwell on it, so she turned her attention back to the ride, her focus sharp and her confidence unshaken.

By the time Brimstone slowed to a controlled canter, she had guided him in a wide, graceful arc, her hands steady on the reins. Her heart swelled with pride as they trotted back toward Julian, who pulled Silverthorne to a halt nearby. The mare's flanks were heaving slightly, but she seemed unbothered, her ears flicking toward Brimstone.

"Well?" Caroline called out, her grin triumphant as she patted the stallion's neck. "Still think I can't manage him?"

Julian dismounted with a fluidity that belied his limp, walking toward her with a measured stride. "What part of 'no faster than a canter' did you fail to understand? His dark eyes were unreadable, but his lips pressed into a thin line. "I'm beginning to think Brimstone has a soft spot for impertinent riders."

"Impertinent, am I?" Caroline laughed, her cheeks warm from the exhilaration of the ride. "You gave me the challenge, Lord Osborne. I merely rose to meet it."

The groom cantered toward them and quickly dismounted, his gaze sweeping over Brimstone, his eyes narrowing slightly as if reassessing Caroline's skill. He gave a slight nod of approval but remained silent.

Julian's gaze softened slightly as he ran a hand down Brimstone's neck, checking the stallion as though to reassure himself the horse was unharmed. "You ride well, Lady Caroline," he said finally, his tone begrudging but sincere.

Caroline almost preened under his mild praise. Not that she wanted to show him such a reaction. "You are surprised?"

"Impressed." Julian gave a quick nod, though his tone remained clipped. "I'll remind you that Brimstone is still my horse."

"Of course." Caroline reached for the reins, preparing to dismount, but Julian was already there. His large hands settled firmly on her waist, halting her movement. His touch sent an unexpected jolt of awareness through her. She stiffened, her breath catching.

"You've proven your point," he said, his voice low, "but allow me."

Before she could protest, he lifted her effortlessly from the saddle. Instinctively, she rested her hands on his shoulders. For a brief, breathless second, they were closer than propriety allowed, closer than to any other man she'd ever known. Her heart thudded in her chest as she caught the faint, woodsy scent of him—leather and cedar mingling with the crisp morning air.

Thank the heavens for gloves, or she may have let her hands linger on his firm chest.

Her boots touched the ground, and she stepped back quickly, smoothing her skirts with deliberate composure as if the motion could erase his unsettling effect on her. It didn't. The lingering warmth of his hands on her waist seemed to radiate through her riding habit.

"Thank you." Somehow, she kept her voice calm and steady though her cheeks warmed. She risked a glance up at him, only to find his dark eyes fixed on her with an intensity that made her pulse skip.

She took another step back, bumping into Brimstone's flank.

He nuzzled her jacket, looking for more carrots and providing a much-needed distraction. "It was a delightful experience. I appreciate you sharing him."

Julian's expression was unreadable as he released Silverthorne's reins to her. "A privilege, Lady Caroline." His tone betrayed no such sentiment.

Caroline turned toward her mare, busying herself with the reins as her heart gradually returned to its normal rhythm. The sensation of his hands lingered, unwelcome and undeniable, and she berated herself silently for the foolish fluttering in her chest.

She straightened her back and fixed her gaze ahead, determined to banish the thoughts that threatened to linger far longer than they should.

Julian touched the back of her hand to get her attention. "I must inform you of something else."

His expression and tone suggested she wouldn't like what he had to say. Caroline took a deep breath. "And what might that be?"

"My father intends to announce our engagement tomorrow."

The words struck like a physical blow. The smile she'd worn so effortlessly faltered, replaced by a look of stunned surprise. "Tomorrow?"

Julian nodded, his stormy eyes intense, but she couldn't hold his gaze. Turning away, she fussed over Silverthorne, the familiar task a shield against the flutter of emotions that threatened to spill over. The exhilaration of the ride drained away, replaced by a nervous energy that coiled tightly in her chest.

She forced a steadying breath, smoothing her expression into one of polite composure before speaking. "I see. Thank you for telling me."

Julian didn't reply, but her skin prickled under the intensity of his gaze. Was he gloating? He'd said he was as much against this arrangement as she was. Well, she refused to give him the satisfaction of any more reaction than she had already displayed.

Instead, she motioned for her groom to assist her, her back straight and her chin high. But Julian stepped forward, his expression unreadable. "Allow me."

She kept her chin raised. "I wouldn't want to trouble you, Lord Osborne. My groom can assist me."

"No doubt," Julian replied smoothly, "but I would like to help you."

Caroline hesitated for a moment before nodding. Her pride warred with practicality. But it would be brutish to push him away and enough people were already watching their encounter.

Julian stepped closer. "Your foot, Lady Caroline."

She placed her boot lightly in his waiting hands, and before she could blink, he lifted her effortlessly into the saddle. She adjusted her seat, smoothing her skirts to avoid meeting his gaze, though her heart gave an inexplicable flutter.

"There." He stepped back. "Not so troublesome after all, was it?"

"Thank you." For some mysterious reason, the urge to tease arose. "I shall remind you of this gallantry the next time you doubt my abilities."

Julian's lips twitched in what might have been the shadow of a smile. "Feel free, Lady Caroline. Though I reserve the right to keep doubting."

She gave him a sidelong glance, brushing a gloved hand over Silverthorne's neck. "I wouldn't expect anything less."

Julian mounted Brimstone with the ease of long practice, his limp barely noticeable as he swung into the saddle.

Eleanor joined them, the two grooms not far behind. "Don't think I missed the headlong gallop you took on that monster of a horse, young lady. We will speak of it later."

Julian turned Brimstone to face them both. "Lady Caroline, Lady Weston, I'll ride back with you. I must speak with Lord Weston."

Caroline's stomach tightened at the mention of Alexander. She didn't need to ask what Julian planned to discuss. The engagement announcement loomed like a storm cloud. She yearned to question him, to demand to know why he was so resigned to this arrangement, but her pride wouldn't allow it.

"Of course." She tilted her chin. "Maybe I will insist on another race."

"You've already won the morning, Lady Caroline. Let's leave it at that."

"That looked thrilling from where I sat." Eleanor tutted, her tone teasing but tinged with warning. "But there will be no more racing in Hyde Park. I suspect the park's early risers may have found it scandalous. Goodness knows who recognised you. Worse still, goodness only knows who will repeat it."

Caroline gave Eleanor what she hoped was a glance full of remorse. "I was merely proving a point, Eleanor. Lord Osborne doubted my riding abilities."

Eleanor raised an eyebrow but refrained from commenting further, though her knowing look spoke volumes.

They set off at a steady pace, the grooms trailing behind. Caroline was hyper-aware of Julian's presence—his strong, steady posture, the faint creak of his saddle, the occasional soft sound of Brimstone's breathing.

Eleanor broke the silence first, her tone light but pointed. "Caroline, you should be more careful. Racing through Hyde Park on a stallion like that—what will people say?"

Caroline glanced sideways at her sister. "If they say anything, it will be about how well I rode."

"Lady Caroline has a point." Julian let out a low chuckle. "Though I suspect my father and brother would have a different opinion."

Caroline stiffened slightly at the mention of the marquess, but she masked it with a breezy laugh. "Your father doesn't strike me as someone who appreciates spontaneity."

Julian's lips quirked into a faint smile, though his eyes remained thoughtful. "No, he doesn't. But he values determination. Perhaps he'll see some merit in your... spirited nature."

Eleanor coughed delicately, clearly holding back a laugh. "Spirited? That's a polite way of putting it."

Julian's gaze lingered on her for a moment, his expression softening. "It's an observation."

The words were simple, but how he said them sent a strange flutter through Caroline's chest. She straightened her shoulders and looked ahead, determined not to let him rattle her further.

As they neared the edge of the park, Eleanor sighed dramatically. "Thank you, Lord Osborne, for bringing Caroline back in one piece."

"Brimstone deserves the credit." Julian's gaze flicked to Caroline. "He seems to have taken a liking to her."

Caroline patted Silverthorne's neck, her voice light. "He has excellent taste."

Julian's faint smile returned, though he said nothing more. The silence that followed was not uncomfortable but charged with tension. As they passed through the gates and returned to the Weston townhouse, her mind churned with thoughts of the impending announcement.

Whatever Julian and Alexander discussed would inevitably shape her future.

Would Alexander ask her opinion?

He didn't have to. The law and custom gave him the right to decide for her. Would Julian even care what she thought of him, of their future together? Or was this simply another duty to him, as it seemed to be for everyone else?

Caroline kept her gaze forward, her expression serene, even as questions and doubts swirled.

Whatever lay ahead, Lord Julian Osborne would not find her an easy match to dismiss.

Chapter Six

The library of the Weston townhouse was quiet, the only sound the steady ticking of the longcase clock in the corner marking the slow passage of time. How long had he been waiting for Alexander? Ten minutes, perhaps? Yet it felt like an eternity.

Julian paced before the fireplace, hands clasped behind his back, the rhythmic click of his boot heels on the polished wood the only other sound in the room. His cane rested against the armchair nearby, close to hand in case he needed it. So far, he'd managed pacing with barely a limp, never mind that his leg pained like the blazes after the morning's escapades in Hyde Park.

He forced himself to stop, resting a hand on the chair's back. Where had his composure gone? The calm, detached resolve he'd cultivated over the years of war and duty had abandoned him.

Lady Caroline Darrow had done what years of horrific war hadn't—she had utterly flustered him.

Every detail of the morning's ride replayed in his mind in a vivid tableau. Where in heaven's name had Lady Caroline learned to ride like that? Her skill as a horsewoman had astonished him. She hadn't merely ridden Brimstone, she had commanded him with a confidence and grace that rivalled the best he'd seen. The sound of her laughter—his new favourite sound in the world—as the stallion thundered ahead still echoed in his mind, refusing to be silenced. She had been fearless, her joy unrestrained, untamed, irrepressible, and entirely herself.

It was maddening. Infuriating. And undeniably compelling.

His hand tightened on the chair, his knuckles whitening. How had his father found the one debutante in London who not only did not bore him but also challenged him at every turn? A wry smile tugged at his lips as he shook his head. The old man had not chosen her for Julian's happiness, that much was certain. Yet, somehow, this arranged match had the makings of something unexpected.

He chuckled softly, then laughed aloud at its absurdity. She had defied him and ignored his warning to keep the pace sedate. Lady Caroline was not the timid debutante he'd anticipated. She was spirited and determined, her horsemanship and evident care for the animals rivalling his own.

It was her spirit that left him uneasy. Her reaction to the news that his father intended to announce their engagement in The Times for all to see had been... troubling, muted. Too muted. He'd expected a reaction, a conversation perhaps. She had been shocked, but her silence afterwards had been far more telling. She had not protested, but neither had she accepted it. And that left him uncertain.

Lady Caroline Darrow was not a woman who could be coerced into compliance. He couldn't shake the feeling that she would resist the arrangement if given the chance. He couldn't let her put everything at risk—his estate, independence, and carefully ordered life.

The door opened, drawing him from his thoughts. Alexander entered, his expression watchful. Julian nodded in greeting and waited for the other man to take the lead.

"Osborne." Alexander gestured toward the armchairs by the fireplace. "Sit. Lady Weston tells me we have much to discuss."

Julian nodded and sat, his posture stiff. He suppressed a grimace as he shifted his leg.

Damn it. If Lady Weston had told Alexander about Caroline's impromptu gallop on Brimstone, Alexander could be about to kick him out. Julian couldn't even complain. He deserved it. Instead, Alexander took the chair opposite, his gaze steady.

The butler entered with a tray of crystal decanters and glasses, carefully setting them down. Alexander poured a generous measure of brandy into two glasses and offered one to Julian.

Julian nodded his thanks, took a mouthful of brandy, and for a moment, enjoyed the burn down his throat and the warmth spreading through his stomach.

Alexander leaned back, every bit the host in charge. "I assume you've spoken with Caroline."

"I have." Julian swallowed again. "She is shocked that Father wants to announce the engagement so soon. His insistence on expedience has left her and us little time to prepare."

Alexander's gaze sharpened. "Are you prepared?"

"Soon, yes. So soon, no. But I could not sway him." Julian frowned. His father's arrogance and stubbornness grated in a way nothing else did or ever had.

Alexander studied him for a moment. "Have you spoken of the marriage, the timing, your living arrangements?"

"We talk about riding." Julian's mouth quirked in a faint smile. "She is ... spirited."

Alexander grimaced. "That's one way of putting it. She's not one to shy away from a challenge."

"No, she isn't." Julian hesitated, considering his words. Should he mention Brimstone at all? Damn it, he was out of practise at polite conversation. "She has strong opinions, and she values her independence. This arrangement is not her choice, but I hoped to find some common values. Her skill as a horsewoman is remarkable. I didn't expect such mastery."

"A sensible course of action. You share a love of riding. It has been Caroline's passion since her first pony as a small child." Alexander's tone softened. "You are right. She is no timid debutante. Not that you would expect such, given her three older sisters."

Having met them at the dinner the night before, Julian could only nod in agreement.

"Few of us are fortunate enough to choose." Alexander shrugged and then he leaned forward. "But I will not force her into this marriage. Caroline's happiness matters to me, and I will not sacrifice it lightly."

Julian's jaw tightened. "I understand and concur. The engagement announcement will have a prominent position in the paper."

Alexander drained his glass and set it down with a quiet clink. "Then understand this—nothing is final until I've spoken with her. If she objects, we will find another solution."

The words landed heavily, though Julian kept his face impassive. Another way? There was no other way. His father had made it clear—marry Lady Caroline Darrow or the estate he cherished would slip from his grasp.

Silence stretched between them. Finally, Julian spoke. "I would like to speak with her before you make any decisions."

"Let me make myself clear, Osborne." Alexander's gaze sharpened. "I do not object to you as a match, not at all. But Caroline's happiness is Lady Weston's primary concern, and it is also mine. Go and speak with her. She's in the small drawing room with Eleanor. Go now. The sooner you address this, the better."

It was the best he could hope for. Julian rose, inclining his head. "Thank you."

He left the library with measured steps, his cane clicking on the tiled floor, his heart a steady drumbeat of apprehension. He didn't relish persuading her, but the alternative was unthinkable. He would not lose his estate after everything he had endured to protect it.

He followed the butler toward the back of the house. The small drawing room was bathed in light from two large windows overlooking the back garden, the delicate furnishings and pale green walls creating an air of calm. Caroline sat by the window, her posture poised as she poured tea for herself and Eleanor. Her riding habit had been replaced by a pale lilac gown, the delicate lace at her wrists and neckline a perfect complement to her fair skin and blue eyes. She looked up as he entered, her expression polite but guarded.

"Lady Caroline." He inclined his head, then turned to Eleanor. "Lady Weston."

Eleanor smiled warmly. "Lord Osborne. Will you join us for tea?"

He hesitated for a fraction of a second before nodding. "Thank you."

Caroline handed him a teacup, her movements graceful but distant.

He took the offered seat across from her, his mind searching for the right words.

"You ride exceptionally well." It was a safe subject to start with. "Brimstone is not an easy mount, yet you managed him with remarkable skill."

Caroline's eyes met his, a flicker of what was hopefully pleasure breaking through her composure. "Thank you. He's a magnificent horse. I enjoyed the challenge."

"I apologise, Lady Weston, for giving you a scare."

Lady Weston—Eleanor—nodded graciously. "Apology accepted, Lord Osborne. The fault is not entirely yours. When Caroline sets her mind on something, she is a monster."

Caroline huffed. "I accept some of the blame, but Brimstone decided to gallop. I just had to hang on and enjoy the ride."

"Enjoy?" Julian's lips quirked in a faint smile. "I was under the impression you thrived on it."

Caroline's cheeks coloured slightly, though her tone remained even. "Perhaps I do. Life without challenges would be unbearably dull, don't you agree?"

Julian's gaze lingered on her, his admiration tempered by a nagging sense of unease. She was clever, confident, and capable of turning this arrangement on its head.

Eleanor set her teacup down. "I'll leave you to discuss whatever it is you came to say, Lord Osborne. Do behave, Caroline."

With a mischievous smile, she rose and left the room, leaving a charged silence in her wake.

Julian shifted, directly meeting Caroline's gaze. "We have much to discuss. The announcement is set for tomorrow. It will change how society sees us. Are you prepared for it?"

Caroline's expression didn't waver, though her grip on her teacup tightened. "No."

He softened his voice. "I assure you. This arrangement need not be a source of conflict."

She arched an eyebrow, her tone laced with irony. "How reassuring."

Julian suppressed a sigh. "I am not blind to your feelings, Lady

Caroline. But I hope you will consider the practical benefits of this match.”

Her eyes flashed, the polite façade slipping for just a moment. “Practical benefits? Is that what you value most, Lord Osborne?”

He met her gaze steadily. “I value stability and honour. And I believe we can find both in this arrangement.”

Caroline set her teacup down, her expression unreadable. “I will consider it. Spend some time considering all those practical benefits.”

Her words, laced with sarcasm, did little to ease his apprehension. Defiance simmered just beneath the surface. She was not a woman to be swayed easily.

What else could he say? He rose to leave, then hesitated, his voice softening. “For what it’s worth, Lady Caroline, I believe we could make this work.”

She looked up at him, her expression unreadable. “We shall see, Lord Osborne.”

So beautiful. So spirited. She felt a draw to him as much as he was drawn to her. He was sure of it.

With a sudden surge of primal instinct, Julian grabbed Caroline by the arm and pulled her forcefully to her feet. She stumbled, caught off guard by his unexpected action. But before she could protest or question his intentions, he cupped her face in his hands and crushed his lips against hers.

Caroline gasped in shock, but it quickly turned into a moan of pleasure as Julian’s tongue delved into her mouth. For a moment, she was frozen, but then something seemed to shift inside her, and she responded eagerly, tangling her fingers in his hair as his body pressed against hers with a desperate need for more.

He was firm yet gentle, determined yet cautious as he relentlessly explored every inch of her mouth. He couldn’t think rationally as their bodies moulded together in an intoxicating dance of desire.

Their kiss deepened, each of them lost in the moment. The heat of Caroline’s body pressed against his, and a thrill coursed through him. He was drawn to her, even though he fought against it.

They finally broke apart, both gasping for air. Her intense gaze speared him to his core. There was no going back. Despite their differences and the conflict of their arranged marriage, an undeniable attraction was pulling them towards each other.

He stepped back. The distance between them was now only inches, but he already missed the warmth of their embrace.

"I...I don't know what came over me." Julian brushed a strand of hair from Caroline's face.

She smiled slightly, still a little breathless. "Perhaps it was just our mutual understanding of this arrangement."

It sounded better than being consumed by lust in the middle of the day in a drawing room with the door ajar. Eleanor wouldn't be far away. Nor would she leave them alone together for much longer.

Julian nodded in agreement before leaning down to capture her lips again. This time, their kiss was more measured but no less passionate.

"I never expected this between us."

Caroline reached up to cup his cheek tenderly. "Neither did I."

They stood there gazing at each other for a long moment before finally pulling away. Would this desire for each other improve the way forward or complicate things further? He pushed the question aside and focused on the present. "May I call on you tomorrow?"

Caroline sat and smoothed her skirt. "You may, though after my morning ride."

Julian smiled. "Perhaps I will see you at the park again."

"Perhaps you will." She shrugged and gave him a cheeky smile through her eyelashes. "I will come prepared with carrots."

The minx.

Eleanor re-entered the room as he was leaving. "Leaving us so soon, Lord Osborne?"

"Unfortunately, I have much to do. Lady Caroline has given me leave to call upon her tomorrow. I will see you then, perhaps."

"Indeed, you will." Eleanor gave him an all-too-knowing smirk.

Julian left the room, his concerns somewhat abated, but his mind was still heavy with uncertainty. One moment of passion did not ensure her commitment to the arrangement—not at all. Convincing her might not be easy, but he had to win—for his future, his estate, and perhaps, just perhaps, the unexpected possibility of something more.

Chapter Seven

Caroline stood at the drawing-room window, fingers pressed against her still-tingling lips. She stared out at the trimmed hedges and blooming rose bushes of the Weston garden, staring yet not seeing.

Three words pulsed through her mind. *He kissed me.* Her chest filled with a strange, breathless excitement at the memory. And not just a kiss. No, it had been deliberate, purposeful, and utterly devastating.

Lord Julian Osborne had kissed her, and she'd kissed him back. Not out of obligation or to play the part of a dutiful fiancée, but because she'd wanted to.

A warm flush crept up her neck. The world had narrowed to the space between them. His firm hands, the warmth of his breath, the steady pressure of his lips against hers, their tongues swirling as if in an unchoreographed dance. She'd expected … what? She had no idea, having never been kissed before. She hadn't anticipated the tenderness. The desire that built within her. The warmth that circled her core. Her pulse quickened again, and she shook her head as if that would be all it took to dislodge the memory.

"Caroline?" Eleanor's voice broke through her reverie. "You've been standing there for an age. What on earth are you thinking about?"

Caroline turned, her cheeks burning as her sister crossed the room with a teasing grin.

"Nothing," she said quickly. Too quickly. She could barely focus on the delicate porcelain cup Eleanor held out to her, the thought of tea forgotten in the chaos of her thoughts.

Eleanor spoke again, her tone full of amusement. "Are you going to drink that tea or simply stare at it until it grows cold?"

Caroline blinked, realising she had taken the cup and clutched it to her chest. She took a hasty sip, the warmth doing little to calm her.

Eleanor laughed. "Nothing? I'll wager that *nothing* involves a certain Viscount Osborne."

Caroline sank into a nearby armchair. "You're impossible."

"And you're smitten." Eleanor dragged the ottoman next to Caroline and plopped down next to her. "Admit it, Caroline. He's not as dreadful as you first thought, is he?"

Truthfully, no, he wasn't. Caroline hesitated to say more, the memory too new, too precious to share.

Eleanor shook her knee. "I'm your big sister. You can't leave me in suspense."

Caroline set down her cup, trying and failing to suppress a shy smile. "He kissed me."

Eleanor gasped, and her hands flew to her mouth. "He didn't!"

"He did. And I..." Caroline pressed her fingertips to her temples. "I didn't stop him."

Eleanor's eyes sparkled with delight. "Tell me everything. Was it romantic? Did he sweep you off your feet? Oh, Caroline, this is wonderful!"

Caroline's cheeks burned hotter. "It was." She paused, gulping as she searched for the right words. "It was delicious."

Eleanor clapped her hands, laughing. "Delicious! Oh, this is better than I imagined. So, how do you feel about him now? Does this mean you're warming to the idea of an engagement?"

"I don't know." Caroline hesitated again. Her heart warred with her head, the exhilaration of the kiss clouding her usual clarity. "He's still a mystery to me, so guarded. But then, there's this other side to him. He's kind to his horses, unexpectedly funny." She broke off, flustered. "I don't know what to think. One moment, he's distant, brooding, and infuriating, and the next—" She paused, exhaling sharply. "The next, he's kissing me as if I'm his anchor in a storm, and I feel as though the ground has been pulled from beneath me."

Eleanor took Caroline's hands in hers. "You're allowed to feel conflicted. This arrangement wasn't your choice, and it was dumped on you on your eighteenth birthday just as you were about to start your season. Perhaps it doesn't have to be so dreadful. He cares for you."

Caroline scoffed. "I doubt that. He's simply fulfilling his duty."

"Are you certain? A man like Julian Osborne doesn't strike me as one to kiss out of obligation." Eleanor arched an eyebrow. "And from how you're blushing, I'd wager you enjoyed it."

Caroline groaned, burying her face in her hands. "I don't know what I feel."

But that was a lie. She'd felt drawn to Lord Osborne. It had been there from the moment they met. If it hadn't been for the marriage contract, courtesy of her late father, he was the kind of man she would have been drawn to in the ballroom.

A knock sounded at the door. Before either of them could respond, Alexander stepped inside and inclined his head. "Eleanor. Caroline. I hope I'm not intruding."

Eleanor rose from the ottoman and settled into the armchair opposite Caroline. "Not at all, darling. It is perfect timing for you to come in and add some practicality to the conversation."

"Let me do exactly that." Alexander pushed the ottoman about halfway between them and sat. "By announcing the engagement in the Times, the marquis is trying to control what we do and how quickly we do it."

Caroline's chest tightened. A creeping sense of panic quickly replaced the excitement of the morning ride and the kiss.

Eleanor frowned. "Isn't it a bit soon for all of this? Caroline hasn't even had time to adjust to the idea."

Caroline stiffened slightly, folding her hands in her lap. "He's trying to force us to arrange a quick wedding, you mean?"

"That's exactly what I mean."

"The bride's family handles the ceremony, the location, the guest list, and the timing. I will not be rushed." Eleanor huffed. "I mean, Caroline will not be rushed."

Alexander laughed.

None of this was putting Caroline at ease. She let out an overly dramatic sigh. "Alice has had three months to organise her wedding, and she is still fussing about details."

Alexander lifted his brow. "Knowing Alice, she will still fuss about her wedding the night before the big event."

"While she is walking down the aisle, most likely." Eleanor chuckled. "I think anything up to six months would be acceptable. We need to book the church and make the other arrangements." Eleanor tapped her finger on her chin. "Mother and Lady Beatrice will help, I'm sure."

Alexander laughed again. "Try and stop them. Remember, Caroline, Julian's father can press for haste all he wants." Alexander emphasised each word. "But the final decision rests with us—well, with you, to be precise."

"He asked leave to call on me tomorrow. Lord Julian, I mean, of course. To discuss things, he said. I guess he meant all the practical arrangements." The practicalities. Caroline knew this couldn't remain in the thrilling realm of stolen kisses and unspoken feelings forever, but a little longer would have been nice.

Alexander nodded. "Not just the wedding, your future residence, the staff you wish to bring with you... These matters need to be agreed upon between you and Osborne."

Caroline's throat tightened. "I haven't even had time to think about it."

"Osborne Hall is in Hertfordshire, close enough to London for convenience but far enough to enjoy the countryside. It's a prosperous estate that is well-managed and well-staffed. Julian resides there rather than in his townhouse in Mayfair, which is quite fashionable, though I gather it's been somewhat neglected. Julian's never been one for the social scene. Perhaps he needs the right lady to bring it to life."

Caroline smiled faintly, the idea of refurbishing a Mayfair townhouse appealing despite her reservations.

"I'm certain he'd be open to living between the two if you desired.

You should ask to see it and decide whether to split your time between London and the estate. Osborne Hall has a full household staff in place, but you're free to bring your additions—ladies' maids, a companion if you wish."

"You will be mistress of two households, Viscountess Caroline." Eleanor squeezed her hand.

Caroline swallowed hard. "It's a great deal to consider."

"I understand. It's overwhelming," Alexander said, his tone kind. "But these are decisions you'll need to make sooner rather than later. Better to argue through your differences now than when you are not situated to your liking after the wedding."

"I can take Nell, can't I?" Caroline couldn't imagine starting her married life with a new maid to break in.

"Of course, darling," Eleanor answered. "You may choose anyone from the staff at all. Jimmy is very good with Silverthorne. He's another you should consider taking."

"Anyone but the cook," Alexander added. "Damn hard to find a decent one during the season in London."

Caroline nodded, though her mind swirled with questions and doubts. "I'll make a list," she said quietly. "It will help me organise my thoughts."

As Alexander left, Caroline remained seated, her thoughts tangled. How could she navigate a future at Osborne Hall, manage a household, and share a life with a man she barely knew?

Eleanor reached for Caroline's hand again, squeezing it reassuringly. "Don't let it overwhelm you, darling. You were born for the role, trained for it, and you are more than capable of handling this."

Caroline managed a faint smile, but the knot in her chest remained. "I need a moment. I think I'll retire to my room."

Caroline leaned back in her chair, the quiet of her room a welcome reprieve after the morning's overwhelming series of events. Her fingertips brushed against her lips, the memory of Julian's kiss vivid and tantalising. A blush crept up her neck, and she pressed her hands to her cheeks as if trying to cool the heat.

"He kissed me," she whispered to the empty room, the words barely audible yet carrying a weight she couldn't ignore. "And it was... delicious."

Her pulse quickened at the memory and how his dark eyes had softened just before his lips met hers. There had been no room for doubt, no hesitation, just a firm, steady certainty that had both thrilled and unnerved her. It was unlike anything she had ever felt before. He had been gentle yet commanding, and she had completely surrendered. If Eleanor hadn't interrupted them, Caroline wasn't entirely sure how far things might have gone.

Sad, but it couldn't all be thrilling kisses. The enormity of her future pressed down on her. The idea of uprooting her life, of stepping into an entirely new role, felt suddenly monumental.

Her maid, Nell, entered with a fresh pot of tea, her cheerful expression a welcome balm to Caroline's frazzled nerves. "You look like you've seen a ghost, miss. Bad news from Lady Eleanor?"

Caroline shook her head, managing a small smile. "Not bad news. I'm overwhelmed, Nell. There's so much to consider, and I don't even know where to begin."

Nell tilted her head. "Sounds like you need one of your lists. Start with what's most important. What's worrying you the most?"

"Should I go ahead with this arrangement? Alexander said he would support me if I wanted to say no. But this marquis sounds like a pompous ass. I bet he would be so angry he'd make the family pay, and if I had to leave England forever? Oh, Nell, I can't do it."

"Sounds like you have answered your question."

"Yeah. I guess so. So, the real question is, do I want to keep fighting against it, or see how we can make it work?"

"Do you like the man?"

Caroline pondered how to put her chaotic thoughts into a simple concept. Not for Nell, more for herself. "I'm drawn to him—he's distant and brooding, yet unexpectedly kind, funny, and capable of kissing me with a passion that leaves me utterly unmoored as if he is both storm and anchor in my life."

Nell sighed, her hand on her heart. "That sounds so romantic. Most importantly, I heard that despite a few shortcomings, you favour him."

"I think you are probably right. Caroline picked up a pen and wrote a heading in her notebook: On Becoming Lady Osborne. "We need to get to know one another better."

"That's what visits and outings are for. Make sure he knows that you want to be courted."

"Courted. I like that idea." Caroline tapped the pen against her chin. "Oh, Nell. Where will we live? You will come with me, won't you? Please say yes. Eleanor said I am to become mistress of two households, Viscountess Osborne. How do I go from the cute, annoying youngest sister to an elegant lady?"

Nell knelt at her feet. "Miss Caroline. Of course, I will come with you. Your dear mother, the dowager countess, is undoubtedly waiting for you to go to her for help. You have three titled sisters who happily manage large households, and Lady Beatrice, bless her sharp tongue, is always ready with advice."

Caroline laughed. "Not necessarily what you want to hear, though."

Nell stood and poured a fresh cup of tea. "Don't forget the wedding itself. That'll be a grand affair, no doubt. You'll need to decide on flowers, a gown, guests..."

Caroline groaned, setting her pen down. "You're not helping, Nell."

"Just keeping you on track, my lady," Nell said with a wink. "But truly, one thing at a time. You've got plenty of sense. You'll manage it all beautifully, and I daresay you'll keep Lord Osborne on his toes."

Caroline's spirits lifted. "You're right. One thing at a time. Thank you, Nell. You've been a great help."

The act of writing calmed her nerves. By the time she finished, she'd filled several pages with notes—practical details to discuss with her family and Lord Julian. These details grounded her and gave her a sense of control over the chaos.

Chapter Eight

The crisp morning air bit at Julian's skin as he rode through Hyde Park, Brimstone's hooves striking a steady rhythm against the dirt path. The park, hushed and bathed in the new morning's golden light, should have offered him peace, but his mind was as far from calm as could be. Every moment of the past few weeks pressed heavily on him. Mostly, his thoughts looped back endlessly to the kiss.

Why had he done it? Or perhaps the better question was, why had he waited so long when he'd wanted to kiss her from the moment she started making friends with Brimstone in his father's stables?

Since first hearing his father's ultimatum, he'd spent most of his time keeping his mind free from any thoughts of marriage. Since meeting Caroline, he'd tried to maintain a distance from her physically and emotionally. Until he kissed her.

A single, impulsive act that unravelled everything.

The ghost of her lips against his, her body soft and yielding, now the memory haunted him. It hadn't been just a kiss, it was an unspoken confession, a crack in the armour he'd worn for so long. What in blazes had possessed him? Years of discipline undone in one moment of weakness. Or was it a weakness?

He wasn't sure anymore. He only knew that in hindsight, it felt both reckless and inevitable at the same time.

He should have kept away until their arranged meeting. Yet here he was, riding through Hyde Park like some lovesick fool, hoping for another glimpse of her on her morning ride. Not that he would admit it to himself—not in so many words. No. He was here because they had arrangements to discuss. That was all. Arrangements, including their engagement, which was blazoned in The Times for the ton to read that very morning. He could repeat it verbatim.

The Marquess of Thornfield is pleased to announce the engagement of his second son, **Viscount Osborne**, *to* **Lady Caroline Darrow**, *fourth daughter of the late Earl of Grantham. The marriage will take place later this season, uniting two esteemed families. Further details will be shared by Lady Caroline's guardians, Viscount and Viscountess Weston, in due course.*

No doubt the last sentence was a dig at Lord Weston to get a move on. But only he knew that his father's ultimatum included a timeline. Six months. The marriage must be within six months, or he lost the estate. He shook his head at himself. Now, he was rambling in his mind.

Then he saw her.

She was ahead on the path, her emerald hat—adorned with an audacious plume—bobbed jauntily in the morning breeze. Even from this distance, her confident posture on horseback was unmistakable.

His pulse quickened. What in blazes was she doing riding alone?

Brimstone responded to the shift in Julian's grip on the reins, his powerful muscles bunching beneath him as they picked up speed. Julian slowed down when he noticed a maid and groom trailing behind her. Not ideal, but not as reckless as he'd first assumed. Still glancing about as if searching for someone, the sight of her set his nerves on edge.

Was she looking for him? He mentally kicked himself for caring so much, though the exhilarating and disconcerting thought continued to gambol in his mind.

She stopped to talk to a young woman, her head tilted and laughter ringing out. But even as she spoke, her gaze kept twitching beyond the woman—searching.

And then she noticed him.

She smiled, a radiant, unguarded smile that caught him entirely off balance. For a moment, the world stilled, and time stopped. The sharp air, the ache in his leg, the restless thrum of his thoughts—none mattered. All that existed was the light in her eyes and the way it reached straight through him.

All he could do was grin back, a foolish grin he couldn't suppress. He rolled his shoulders back. *Damn it, man, get hold of yourself.*

He approached deliberately, straightening his posture to mask the tumult inside. The woman she spoke with, noticing the direction of Caroline's gaze, gave her a knowing smirk before excusing herself.

"Lady Caroline." He inclined his head as he slowed Brimstone's pace to match hers. "Out for another morning ride, I see."

"I find it clears the mind," Her steady gaze, so direct and unapologetic, seemed to bore into his very soul. "Do you not agree?"

Julian nodded, though his mind was not clear when she was near. "Indeed. Though I suspect my reasons for riding are different from yours."

Her lips curved faintly, the hint of a challenge in her eyes. "Perhaps. Shall we see if our paths align?"

He couldn't deny her, even if he'd wanted to. "Very well."

They rode side by side in silence for a moment, the tension between them as taut as a drawn bowstring. But it was a different kind of tension now, that neither seemed willing to acknowledge. Was she as affected by the kiss as he was?

"You ride well," Julian said after breaking the silence. "Better than most men I've known."

Caroline glanced at him, her lips twitching with amusement. "I'll take that as a compliment, though I suspect it's faint praise."

"Not at all faint, Lady Caroline. Earned."

"You were surprised though, weren't you? Admit it." Her eyes gleamed with mischief. "Did you believe I would be a helpless novice?"

"Hardly." He chuckled, thinking of how she had won Brimstone over with carrot pieces and the right amount of praise. "But Brimstone is no ordinary mount. Not many would have managed him so confidently."

The brief flush of pride in her cheeks made his chest ache in an unfamiliar, unsettling way. She was captivating, not just in her beauty but in her defiance, spirit, and refusal to be anything less than herself.

It was precisely those qualities that made it so difficult for him to keep his distance.

He broke the silence again. "I couldn't help but notice that you were riding alone."

Her smile faded, replaced by a steely glint in her eyes. "I am not alone. Nell and Jerry are right behind me. Besides, I am quite capable of taking care of myself."

"I'm sure you are." Julian flicked his gaze to the maid and groom, trailing far too distantly for his liking. "However, I would prefer you not test the limits of that capability. Your servants are far enough behind to be useless if trouble finds you."

Caroline gazed back at her servants, her gaze narrowing. "Are you chastising me, Lord Osborne?"

Julian kept his expression calm, though a hint of frustration escaped in his tone. "I am simply offering advice to ensure your safety. Your maid and groom are too far behind."

Caroline's jaw tightened. "I assure you, here in Hyde Park, I am perfectly safe."

"Hyde Park is not without hazards, even for a skilled horsewoman." Julian's gaze remained steady. "Humour me, Lady Caroline."

With a sigh, Caroline took off in a fast walk. She gave a sharp and unladylike whistle, calling her maid and groom to catch up. Julian fell into step beside her again, his pulse still unsteady. Had he overstepped? Her stiff posture suggested he had.

When they returned to the park's entrance, their charged silence had grown almost unbearable. Julian's mind churned with conflicting emotions. She was infuriating, unpredictable, and yet utterly irresistible.

As they approached the Weston townhouse, her scowl deepened. He hated the loss of her smile, hated that he had been the cause of it.

"Forgive me, Lady Caroline." He softened his tone." Honestly, I am unused to polite company and perhaps a little too familiar with barking orders at my troops. I need to master conversation without sounding like a drill sergeant.

Caroline huffed though her glare softened. "I suppose even a drill sergeant can learn."

The rest of the ride passed in uncomfortable silence, and by the time they reached the Weston townhouse, Julian wasn't sure if he was still permitted to call on her. Had he pushed her too far? Was she angry enough to refuse their upcoming discussion altogether?

Caroline answered the question when she said. "The stables are this way." And led him to the well-appointed barn not far from the house.

His groom dismounted quickly and took charge of Brimstone. Caroline's groom did the same with her horse. He was gratified that she had no qualms about using the back door, and Julian followed her inside.

Her stride was as confident as ever, but her shoulders were stiff, which made his chest tighten with unease.

He followed her inside, bracing himself for whatever lay ahead. He'd need every ounce of whatever composure he had left now.

Chapter Nine

"Whatever has that poor riding habit done to you?" Eleanor barged into Caroline's bedroom, her tone half exasperated, half amused.

"Nothing." Caroline delivered a half-hearted kick at the discarded emerald hat she'd worn that morning.

Nell, ever efficient, darted in and collected the hat before it could suffer further indignity. She cast a wary glance at Caroline, now pacing like a caged tiger.

"You marched into the house with a face like thunder." Eleanor had no intention of leaving Caroline to her sulking. She settled herself on the edge of the bed. "Then you shoved poor Lord Osborne into the drawing room as if he were peddling second-rate wares. What on earth happened?"

"Poor Lord Osborne." Caroline balled her hands into fists on her hips. "That man! That man is impossible."

Eleanor tilted her head, her brow lifted, and lips pursed as she observed Caroline's restless movements. "Well? Are you going to tell me, or must I guess?"

"Do you know what he said to me?" Caroline stopped mid-pace, spun towards her sister and mimicked Julian's deep baritone. "I couldn't help but notice that you were riding alone. Can you imagine? As if I haven't been riding for years without tumbling off my horse like some green girl. I told him that I can take care of myself."

Eleanor's eyes narrowed. "You rode alone in Hyde Park?"

"You aren't listening to me." Caroline stamped her foot. "Nell and Jerry were right behind me."

"Didn't Lord Osborne see them?"

Caroline turned away from Eleanor. "Nell, I will wear my pink visiting dress."

That man did not deserve to see her in one of her lovely new outfits. The old pink monstrosity would do just fine. Caroline swallowed a hard lump in her throat. Nell and Jerry had fallen behind, but she didn't want to get either of them in trouble. She considered her words carefully. "He saw them. He didn't like the distance between us. Not that it's—"

"Nell," Eleanor said crisply. "a word if you please."

"Yes, my lady." Nell was already on her way back into the room, and she folded Caroline's gown carefully across the back of the seat before giving a small curtsy before Eleanor.

"You accompanied Miss Caroline on her ride this morning. Is that correct?"

Nell hesitated, darting a quick, apologetic glance at Caroline.

"Did you and the groom fall behind at any point?"

"We did, my lady, it was but for a moment. Jerry's horse stumbled over a fallen log, and he dismounted to inspect the horse's leg. Miss Caroline was talking with Miss Alice then, and I didn't wish to interrupt." Nell stopped speaking, her breathing fast.

"And then?" Eleanor prompted.

"Then Lord Osborne arrived." Nell's voice faltered as she wrung her hands. "They set off at quite a brisk pace. We caught up as quickly as we could."

In the silence that followed, she realised the reality of the situation. Even for a moment, a woman alone in such a public place could quickly become gossip fodder.

Caroline drew closer to her maid. "You aren't in any trouble, Nell. It is my fault. I should have turned for a moment to ensure you and Jerry were still following. I didn't even realise the horse was harmed. Is he alright?"

Nell nodded before Eleanor dismissed her. Nell retreated to the dressing room, her cheeks flushed.

Eleanor turned that no-nonsense gaze onto Caroline. "You promised Alexander."

Caroline sank into a chair, her anger giving way to guilt. "I kept my promise. I took Nell and Jerry with me. I-I didn't look back. It looks like Lord Osborne was within his rights to chastise me."

"As your fiancé, indeed he was. Eleanor exhaled slowly. "If Alexander finds out, he will return Silverthorne to the estate."

"Please don't tell him," Caroline whispered, her voice cracking. "I couldn't bear it."

Eleanor studied her for a long moment. "Very well. On one condition."

"Anything."

"You will apologise to Lord Osborne for behaving like a spoiled child."

Caroline grimaced but nodded. "I will. I was cool to him, and now I realise he was only looking out for my reputation and safety."

Eleanor's stern expression softened. "Good. Now dress, smooth your ruffled feathers, and meet him like the future viscountess you are."

It wasn't until she was dressed and her soft curls pinned up that she realised Nell had ignored her demand for the old pink and dressed her in one of her newest day dresses. The lightweight muslin of dusky pale yellow, decorated with dainty pink flowers, was perfect for daytime elegance. With the matching fitted Spencer jacket in pale pink and pale cream gloves, she was ready to descend the stairs as any future viscountess might.

When Caroline went downstairs, she found the drawing-room empty. The butler knocked on the open door. "Lady Caroline, Lord Weston took Lord Osborne to his study. I will let his lordship know you are ready to receive him."

Eleanor joined her with a basket of embroidery. "I am your chaperone this morning—"

"But we are—"

"Yes, I am aware that you are engaged. However, the announcement was only made this morning, and we have yet to present you socially as an engaged couple."

Caroline huffed and slid onto the chaise lounge.

"For heaven's sake, Caroline, have you remembered nothing that I taught you?"

Caroline stiffened at the rebuke but adjusted her posture and rang for tea. She pulled out her notebook and reread the notes she had made, all the things she wanted to discuss with Lord Osborne. She felt like adding that she was not to be ordered around like a soldier by a drill sergeant, but that was not something she would mention in front of Eleanor, if at all.

Caroline glanced at the steadily ticking clock on the mantel. It felt like an age, but she had been waiting only for minutes. Smoothing her skirt for what must have been the fourth time, she clutched her notebook tightly in her gloved hands.

Eleanor sat nearby, her embroidery hoop in hand. "Relax, dearest," she said without looking up. "He's not here to deliver a battle report."

"No, he's here to discuss arrangements." Caroline tightened her fingers on the notebook. "Our future. Our life together. What if he dismisses everything I've prepared?"

Eleanor smiled faintly. "If he does, I'll intervene. Now, breathe. You're holding that notebook as though you mean to fend him off with it."

Caroline loosened her grip slightly. She reminded herself this was a business meeting, though the rapid fluttering of her heart betrayed her nerves. He might dismiss her thoughts without showing any emotion, and his reserved nature made him infuriatingly challenging to read at times.

The door creaked open, and Julian stepped inside. Still in his riding attire, his confident presence seemed to fill the room. His gaze settled on her, dark and intent, and Caroline's breath hitched for a moment.

"Lady Caroline, Lady Weston." He inclined his head. "Thank you for receiving me."

Caroline rose and curtsied, the action as much to steady her nerves as to observe propriety. "Lord Osborne. Thank you for staying. We have much to discuss."

"Indeed." He gestured for her to resume her seat and took the armchair opposite. He lay his folding cane against the chair, careful to make sure it was within easy reach, though he betrayed no sign of discomfort.

"Does your leg hurt after riding?" she blurted out, curiosity and concern overriding her training to avoid personal matters at all costs.

"Unfortunately, yes. But it doesn't stop me from riding. Though some people complain that riding stops me from doing other things."

He spoke with a smile in his tone, but Caroline was prepared to bet it was his stern-faced father who complained the most.

At a rather pointed glance from Eleanor, Caroline folded her notebook. "I have made some notes, Lord Osborne. But first, I must apologise." She met Julian's gaze directly. "For my behaviour this morning. You were right to chastise me."

Julian blinked, clearly caught off guard. "Thank you, Lady Caroline, and I apologise for my unnecessary gruffness."

The use of her name, spoken in his deep, steady voice, sent an unexpected warmth through her. She took a deep breath, then another, forcing herself to stay composed.

Eleanor poured tea, breaking the tension. "Now that apologies are exchanged, shall we begin? Caroline, you've prepared notes."

Julian held up his palm to stop her. "May I call you Caroline now that we are engaged and about to discuss arrangements?"

A blush of pleasure climbed into Caroline's cheeks. "Please do, and may I call you Julian?"

"Nothing would please me more." His face broke into a smile that set Caroline's stomach aflutter, and suddenly, everything was right with the world. Unfortunately, with Eleanor in the room, there would be no more delicious kisses.

They drank tea and politely chatted about the weather and the people they knew until Julian pointed at Caroline's notebook and said, "You made notes."

Caroline opened to the first page. "I have some questions and thoughts on the various practical matters we must address."

His lips quirked in the faintest of smiles. "A thorough approach. I expected nothing less."

"First, the wedding arrangements. Have you any preferences as to timing?"

"None." Julian leaned back. "Though my father would prefer expedience."

"Of course, he would." Caroline's tone was dry before she caught herself. She cleared her throat. "I thought late summer would be suitable—allowing time for preparations but avoiding the crowded months of the season." And time for them to get to know one another better, she thought but didn't add.

"So, within three months. A practical choice." Julian seemed pleased as he nodded.

Before Caroline could continue, Eleanor interrupted. "If I may butt in, Alexander and I would love to host your engagement ball in a week or so's time. A small gathering of family and close friends."

Caroline couldn't believe she'd forgotten such an important point. She cast Eleanor a grateful smile before moving on. "Next, the question of our residence. I understand Osborne Hall is your primary estate, but you also own a townhouse in London?"

"I do," he said, his expression neutral. "It's well situated in Mayfair, though I've found little reason to use it since returning from the war."

Caroline hesitated. "Would you be amenable to dividing our time between the estate and London during the season?"

Julian's expression cooled slightly. "Osborne Hall is my home—our home. The townhouse is functional but hardly necessary."

Caroline bristled. "Hardly necessary? It's well situated, and maintaining a social presence is not trivial."

Julian leaned forward, his jaw tightening. "Osborne Hall is more than suitable for entertaining. If presence is required, we can visit as needed."

"My sisters and many nieces and nephews will all be in London during the season. We are close ..." Caroline gulped in some air. This conversation had gone off the rails, and she wasn't sure how to get it back on track.

Eleanor coughed delicately. "Family is important, Lord Osborne.

Perhaps a compromise? Divide the season evenly—a few weeks at Osborne Hall, a few in London."

Caroline's gaze darted to Julian, her pulse quickening. He stared into the fire for several long moments. His expression was inscrutable. To her immense relief, he nodded. "An equitable solution. Though Osborne Hall will remain our primary home."

"I understand." Breath hitching, she glanced at her list. "I'm sure Osborne Hall has a full complement of staff, but perhaps I could address staffing in the townhouse, and I would like to bring my lady's maid and perhaps one or two additional attendants."

"That's reasonable." Julian nodded. "The townhouse will need redecorating, something I will leave entirely to you."

Caroline had half expected this, so she did not choke on her tea at the thought of the responsibility. Before she could move to her next point, Julian spoke again.

"I know the season is brimming with social engagements, but I would love you to visit Osborne Hall. Perhaps for a weekend, with suitable chaperones, of course."

"I couldn't think of anything nicer." Eleanor rang the bell for fresh tea and cake. "Caroline, perhaps Mother, will accompany us."

Julian inclined his head. "I have been remiss, Lady Weston. I have not yet called on the Dowager Countess."

"Eleanor, please. We are to be family. Mother has been visiting our sister, Olivia, to help with the twins now that Olivia is with child again. But she will return for the engagement celebration."

Caroline wished she could visit Julian alone, but Alexander would never permit it. Given his gentlemanly conduct, she couldn't imagine Julian permitting it either. Still, a chaperoned visit would be fun. She came out of her reverie to find Julian watching her with amusement and Eleanor with her brow lifted.

She quickly checked her notes, but she did not need them now. Much of what she had written were minor details they could sort out later. The only other important considerations were her horses and the grooms they were familiar with.

Julian's thoughtful responses and occasional flashes of dry humour reminded her of the man she had glimpsed in quieter moments—the one who cared deeply about his estate and took pride in its success.

When they reached the end of her list, Julian leaned forward slightly. "You've given these matters considerable thought. I commend your diligence."

Colour rose to her cheeks, but Caroline kept her tone light. "I simply wish to ensure that our future is as seamless as possible."

"Seamless?" His lips twitched. "An ambitious goal. But one worth striving for."

Their eyes met, and the air between them felt charged for a moment. Julian's expression softened. He kept the man behind the reserved and confident exterior well hidden. Was he as composed as he appeared? No. She'd seen the hints of vulnerability. There was more to him than met the eye.

"I've taken enough of your time." Julian stood and bowed. "Your thoroughness is appreciated."

"Let me get my social diary." Eleanor graciously left the room, leaving the door just slightly ajar.

Caroline stood, smoothed her skirts and stepped closer to him. "Thank you so much for the invitation to visit your estate, Julian. I can't wait to see it."

He took her hands in his. "I hope you will love it as much as I do."

"I'm sure Silverthorne and I will be pleased." She gazed into his eyes, wanting him to kiss her, but not brave enough to make the first move.

Finally, he lowered his lips to hers and brushed the briefest kisses across them. Not enough. But Eleanor was returning to the room. Julian stepped back and kissed the back of her hand as Eleanor returned with the diary.

Caroline could hardly think straight. He and Eleanor settled on a date, just over a week away, to present them to society as a betrothed pair and the following weekend for their visit to Osborne Hall.

He shot her a bemused smile as he left, and the tension between her shoulders eased as satisfaction surged through her. This meeting, though daunting, had proven that they could work together. Caroline's heart raced, not with fear or uncertainty, but with the strange, exhilarating sense that they might succeed at forging something more than a mere arrangement.

Chapter Ten

The day of her engagement ball had finally arrived. Caroline stood on the small balcony overlooking the ballroom, a murmured symphony of conversation and laughter rising to meet her. Her breath caught as she gazed at the mirrored walls reflecting the swirling colours of elegant gowns and quality evening wear.

Her reflection stared back, a vision transformed by the modiste's deft hands. The gown was a masterpiece of pale green silk, its bodice adorned with delicate pearl embroidery that shimmered faintly in the flickering light of chandeliers. The soft, flowing skirts, edged with delicate silver lace, whispered with every movement, lending her a regal air that belied the turmoil within.

"Perfect." Eleanor stepped back to admire her handiwork. She adjusted the diamond necklace that nestled just below Caroline's collarbone. The stones caught the light, casting tiny stars across the satin fabric.

Caroline touched the pendant lightly. "It was Mama's. She said she wanted me to have it for my engagement."

Eleanor smiled. "She couldn't have chosen better. It's exquisite, and it suits you perfectly."

Caroline brushed her fingers over the delicate tiara, anchoring her upswept curls. The pearls and diamonds gleamed with an ethereal radiance, echoing the embroidery on her gown. "Thank you for this," she murmured.

Eleanor kissed her cheek. "Now stop fidgeting. You look perfect, and tonight is about celebration, not apprehension."

Caroline attempted a smile, though her stomach churned. "Easy for you to say. You're not the one whose name is being whispered by half the ton."

Eleanor squeezed her hand reassuringly. "They're whispering because they're envious. And because you've managed to land a viscount with more brooding charm than they could dream of."

Caroline gave a dry laugh. "If only they knew that this is a marriage arrangement."

Eleanor puffed out a breath. "At least half the marriages in this room were arranged. From what I see, you and Julian have something far more promising than most."

She did like him, rather a lot. His reserved nature intrigued her, and his moments of dry humour or quiet thoughtfulness caught her off guard in the best way. Since discussing their future, he'd called on her most days and taken her on carriage rides and to the opera. Or they just sat and talked, mostly about horses. But that was okay, they loved and enjoyed riding the creatures.

The butler's arrival interrupted her thoughts. "The Marquess of Thornfield and Viscount Osborne have arrived."

Caroline's pulse quickened as Julian entered the ballroom. His tall frame commandingly dominated the room. Dressed impeccably in dark evening wear, he exuded a quiet authority that silenced the low murmur of conversation.

His gaze lifted as if drawn by hers, and their eyes locked. Julian gave her a faint nod, his expression unreadable, but something flickered in his eyes—a spark that sent warmth flooding her.

Eleanor caught Caroline's arm as she made to descend the stairs. "Alexander will walk you downstairs and make the announcement."

"Now?" Caroline's throat tightened. She'd hoped for some time alone with Julian before the inevitable spectacle.

Eleanor nodded. "Come, Alexander is waiting for us on the landing."

The ballroom thrummed with anticipation as Caroline descended on Alexander's arm, each step deliberate. Her serene smile masked the riot of nerves beneath. The air was thick with the weight of expectation, and every whisper and glance added to the pressure.

"Deep breaths," Alexander murmured. "You'll do wonderfully."

Near the foot of the staircase, Julian stepped forward to join them. He bowed slightly, his gaze steady, and murmured, "You are radiant."

Caroline inclined her head, her cheeks warming. "Thank you, Julian."

Alexander cleared his throat, drawing the attention of the room. The chatter quieted, and all eyes turned toward him.

"Ladies and gentlemen." Alexander's baritone voice carried effortlessly. "It is my pleasure to formally announce the engagement of my dear sister-in-law, Lady Caroline Darrow, to Viscount Osborne."

A murmur of approval rippled through the crowd, punctuated by scattered applause. Caroline felt the weight of every gaze, though she held her head high, her smile unwavering.

Julian drew a small velvet box from his pocket. When he opened it, gasps were audible. Nestled within was a delicate band of gold set with a single enormous sapphire flanked by two sparkling diamonds.

"This ring belonged to my grandmother." Julian's voice was tinged with emotion. It is a symbol of love and commitment, passed down through generations. Lady Caroline, it is my honour to offer it to you."

Caroline could not find words. Her breath caught as he slipped the ring onto her finger. It fit perfectly, and its weight was both grounding and exhilarating. She looked up at him, her heart full, and found his gaze fixed on her with an intensity that sent a warm thrill through her.

Guests cheered, and a line quickly formed as guests approached to offer congratulations, their words a mix of genuine warmth and thinly veiled curiosity. Fragments of conversation floated around her, some innocuous, others sharp-edged. Caroline endured it with wells of grace she hadn't realised she possessed, though her nerves frayed with each passing moment.

The music swelled, and the first dance was announced. As the betrothed couple, it was their duty to lead.

"Caroline." Julian extended his arm, and she took it, grateful for the excuse to escape the throng.

"You're doing well," he murmured as they moved toward the dance floor. "Better than I am."

"Is that a compliment?"

He glanced down at her, a faint smile ghosting across his lips. "Take it as you will."

Julian guided her onto the floor with practised ease, one hand firmly against her back.

"Smile," Julian murmured under his breath, his tone as calm and steady as his arm beneath her hand.

"I am smiling," she hissed back through gritted teeth.

Julian turned his head slightly, his lips quirking into the faintest hint of amusement. "Ignore all the gossip, my dear. They do not matter."

Despite her nerves, Caroline felt a strange sense of comfort in his presence, as though his steadiness would anchor her, whatever the circumstances.

"Are you ready for the scrutiny?" he asked softly.

"I suppose I have no choice." She met his gaze. "Are you?"

His smile deepened, though it didn't quite reach his eyes. "I've had years of practice being scrutinised. You'll find I'm quite adept at ignoring it."

Some people might find the waltz scandalous, but it became her haven. Eleanor had worn down Alexander's resistance until he agreed to include several in the evening's programme. Her triumph tasted of rebellion wrapped in silk.

Snug in Julian's arms, they moved across the polished floor, her heart thundering though her face betraying nothing but serene confidence. Beneath the precise steps roiled something raw and dangerous. Alexander's hand at her waist burned through layers of fabric, the pressure both her anchor and a torment.

The assembled crowd watched them with hungry eyes. They were the picture of society's aspirations—his ancestral bloodline matching her impeccable connections, their combined fortunes enough to gild gossip. Yet a real connection sparked in the space between their bodies, even though they carefully maintained the precise distance dictated by propriety.

How his fingers lingered a fraction too long at her waist, how the flush at her throat couldn't be blamed entirely on exertion, how their eyes met with a frequency that stretched the boundaries of decorum... all of it be dissected over teacups and during carriage rides, no doubt for several days. At that moment, Caroline didn't care.

Caroline found herself the centre of attention, a steady stream of guests wanting to dance with her. When she stopped for a short break, alone against the wall, every whisper from the crowd seemed to cut through her confidence.

"Why the rush, do you think?" a woman murmured behind her. "They've barely courted."

"Perhaps Lady Caroline is not as blameless as she appears." The reply came with a sharp laugh. "The Thornfields may have had no choice."

Caroline stiffened. Her engagement to Julian was never going to escape the ton's scrutiny, but the unexpected direct insinuation cut her to the quick. She searched the crowd for one of her sisters or Julian, but no one was nearby. Her composure wavered until a familiar voice cut through the din.

"Well, if they're gossiping, you must be doing something right," Lady Beatrice declared as she approached.

Caroline exhaled, grateful for her presence. "They're dreadful."

Lady Beatrice waved a gloved hand as if swatting at a fly. "Let them prattle. Half these people don't have the brains the good Lord gave a goose. Focus on keeping your spine straight and your smile sweet. It unnerves them."

Caroline smiled despite herself. "You make it sound so easy."

"It is." Lady Beatrice's eyes twinkled with mischief. "Especially when you know the right targets." She raised her voice. "Look there, the Duchess of Harwick. She dresses her age, bless her, but it's an age no one else remembers."

Caroline choked back a laugh. Lady Beatrice continued, her sharp gaze scanning the room, "And there's Lord Catherby—more interested in his neighbour's wine cellar than his wife."

"Lady Beatrice!" Caroline whispered, scandalised but amused.

Lady Beatrice smirked. "I've survived forty-odd London seasons, my dear. You learn where to aim."

As they moved through the crowd, congratulations mingled with whispers. Caroline caught fragments of conversation, some innocuous, others biting.

"They say he's a recluse. Barely sets foot in London."

"I heard she galloped across Hyde Park like a common hussy. It's such a spirited match for such a brooding man. I wonder how long this happy phase will last?"

"And her dowry? I had no idea Thornfield was in such dire need as to choose an unknown chit for his second son."

The woman who spoke the words suddenly paled and disappeared into the crowd. Caroline felt his presence and turned to face a glowering Julian. He glanced down at her, and his expression softened. "Ignore them."

"Easier said than done," she murmured.

"Come." He nudged her to a quieter corner of the room. "I won't have you upset by their nonsense."

In the relative quiet, Julian blew out a sigh of exasperation. "I expected gossip, but I hadn't realised it would be this vile."

Caroline forced a smile. "It's part of the game. Let them talk. I'm learning to aim."

Julian raised an eyebrow. "Aim?"

"Advice from Lady Beatrice." She smiled despite her soured mood. "I am to find the right moment, aim and fire a barb in return."

"She's a formidable ally. Remind me never to cross her." Julian chuckled, the sound low and warm.

Caroline tugged him to the open French windows. "Let's find some peace in the garden."

The night air whispered sweet promises against her heated skin as they escaped the suffocating brilliance of the ballroom.

They found sanctuary behind a towering marble urn spilling over with night-blooming jasmine. Its heady perfume was intoxicating and its vibrant growth effectively shielded them from prying eyes. Alexander's hand found hers, his fingers trembling slightly against her gloved palm. Caroline's breath hitched at this revelation of vulnerability, and she was undone.

Her body swayed toward his with the inevitability of the tide answering the moon.

Alexander traced the edge of her jaw with his fingertips, the gesture achingly gentle.

When their lips met, it was not the fierce clash of unbridled passion that Caroline had expected. Instead, it was a slow melting of all the boundaries between them, his mouth soft against hers, tasting of wine and possibility. Her fingers curled into the fine wool of his coat, anchoring herself against the sensation of falling.

She lost track of how long they spent entwined in one another's arms, but the sound of approaching voices shattered their sanctuary. They parted reluctantly; something fundamental had shifted, and the arrangement had transformed into something tangible.

They whirled back into the ballroom as the musicians started a spirited country dance. Dozens of calculating gazes settled upon Caroline, no doubt each seeking to divine the truth behind her windswept appearance, the loosened curls brushed against her flushed neck. She silently prayed they would attribute her heightened colour to nothing more than vigorous dancing. Yet a part of her thrilled at the secret warmth of knowing otherwise, even as she arranged her features into practised innocence.

The evening had unfurled like the Bayeux Tapestry, a story of whispered speculation and meaningful glances. Each time someone murmured about their engagement—some with approval, others with barely concealed disdain—Caroline was drawn to Julian's steady presence across the room. Their eyes would meet over the rim of a wine glass, across a cluster of chattering guests, and in those fleeting moments of silent communion, something profound took root. Every arch comment from the dowagers and every sharp glance from former friends only strengthened the gossamer threads binding them together. Their shared secret became a shield against society's barbs.

When the orchestra started the opening notes of the final waltz, exhaustion settled over Caroline like a heavy cloak. She stifled a yawn behind her fan even as her heart quickened at Julian's approach. He extended his hand with quiet assurance, and the familiar warmth of his touch sent a current of awareness through her tired limbs.

Julian led her to the dance floor, and as they moved together, the weight of the evening seemed to lift, replaced by the growing certainty that each challenge ahead would find them standing as one, their alliance forged this evening in this ballroom under the ton's unwitting gaze.

Chapter Eleven

A sharp knock at the door roused Julian from his restless sleep. He blinked groggily as Finch entered, carrying a tray laden with steaming coffee, buttered toast, and a small stack of envelopes tied with a neat ribbon.

"Good morning, Colonel." Finch set the tray on the bedside table and handed Julian the ribboned stack. "The post arrived early. Most appear to be congratulatory notes."

Julian propped himself up against the pillows, suppressing a groan as the tension in his hips and shoulders reminded him of the previous night's waltzes. "Congratulatory? Or thinly veiled attempts to secure an invitation to Osborne Hall?"

"A fair mix, I'd wager." Finch's tone was as dry as ever, though his eyes glinted with amusement.

Julian reached for the coffee, taking a long sip as Finch tidied the room with his usual efficiency. One envelope caught Julian's eye—a gold-embossed card from a dowager known for her excessive flattery. He opened it, skimming her effusive praise of the match and unsubtle mention of her unmarried niece.

"Tedious." He tossed it onto a growing pile on the floor.

Finch deftly retrieved the cards and set them aside before returning to Julian. "I will ask the steward to deal with them when we get home. Downstairs hasn't gossiped this much in years. The staff are abuzz with talk of Lady Caroline and her family."

Julian quirked an eyebrow, intrigued despite himself. "Oh? What have you gleaned from your network of spies?"

Finch placed a folded shirt into the wardrobe, his expression unperturbed. "Only what the footmen have told the housemaids. It seems Lady Caroline and her sisters are a lively bunch. The matriarch, Lady Beatrice, is known for her sharp tongue and an even sharper eye for impropriety. She reduced a duchess to silence once over a poorly chosen bonnet."

Julian smirked. "Having met the dowager, I can imagine the scene."

"Lady Eleanor is said to manage her household with a firm yet kind hand. She's highly regarded by her staff, who admire her efficiency and warmth."

Julian nodded, his mind wandering briefly to the easy camaraderie he'd observed between Caroline and her sisters and brothers-in-law. It was a dynamic unlike anything he'd experienced in his own family, free from the stifling formality that often defined his interactions with his father and brother.

"And Lady Caroline herself?" He feigned indifference as he reached for another letter.

Finch paused, his expression briefly contemplative. "She's spoken of with fondness, Colonel. The staff say she's spirited and kind, particularly fond of her many horses. They find her refreshing, though perhaps a touch headstrong."

"A touch?" Julian chuckled, shaking his head. "You're being charitable, Finch."

"Merely repeating what I've heard." Finch's lips twitched with the hint of a smile. "Though I dare say headstrong qualities have their uses."

Julian set down the last letter—a perfunctory note from an old family acquaintance—and leaned back against the pillows. "It's strange, Finch. I envied her family last night amidst all the frivolity and whispers. The warmth, the banter, and even the chaos starkly contrasted to Thornfield House."

Finch's movements slowed for just a moment.

Julian gazed at the ceiling, his thoughts drifting to Caroline, her laughter, her quick wit, the way she'd handled the whispers with a grace that belied her frustration—all of it brought home how lucky he had been to find her. "She'll bring life to Osborne Hall," he said finally.

Finch straightened. "I believe she will. And perhaps more than that."

Julian didn't respond. Instead, he reached for his coffee again.

"If you've no further need of me, Colonel, I'll prepare your bags for Osborne Hall."

Julian nodded absently, his gaze distant. "Thank you, Finch."

As the door clicked shut behind his manservant, Julian reflected that Thornfield House, with all its grandeur and history, felt hollow in a way that the Weston townhouse never did. Perhaps it wasn't the house itself, but what it represented—a legacy built on duty and expectation, devoid of the warmth and connection he now realised he craved.

With a determined exhale, he swung his legs over the side of the bed and reached for his clothes. It was time to return to Osborne Hall, and time to confront the possibilities that came with a life shared with Lady Caroline Darrow.

Julian limped down the stairs. He'd have to travel home in the carriage. He would not make the trip safely with his leg paining like this. A heavy oak door closed somewhere in the house, the resounding thud an unpleasant reminder of a gunshot. The echo reverberated through the vast, cold entryway, where no welcoming hum of family life greeted him. Instead, the staff moved in silence, efficient and deferential, a sharp contrast to Alexander's townhouse's lively, warm chaos.

The vibrant laughter and teasing of Caroline's sisters and Caroline's radiant smile all seemed like a fairy tale in this sombre house where duty reigned supreme. He paused in the grand hall, staring at the ancestral portraits lining the walls. Generations of Thornfields glared down, their expressions unyielding, their eyes full of the same weight he'd carried since he was a boy.

Would Caroline feel this same chill when she entered as Viscountess Osborne?

He clenched his jaw and strode toward the study, his cane tapping softly against the polished floors. His father had summoned him to present himself before he left. Another impending conversation about duty, no doubt as if duty hadn't governed every decision he'd ever made.

Except kissing Caroline. Duty had been the last thing on his mind in that impulsive act.

Julian entered the marquess' study without waiting to be announced. His father sat at his imposing mahogany desk, the morning light casting harsh lines across his stern face.

"You're late." The marquess did not bother to look up from a stack of correspondence.

Julian sank into the chair opposite his father. "I had a large number of cards requiring a response."

"As do I." The marquess finally looked up, his gaze sharp and appraising. "It was a well-executed affair." His smirk became greedy. "Lord Weston appears to be even wealthier than I thought."

Julian pursed his lips. He would not discuss his soon-to-be brother-in-law's wealth in any way. "Lady Caroline handled the evening gracefully despite the inevitable scrutiny."

The marquess leaned back in his chair, steepling his fingers. "Good. She'll need that resilience to navigate her role in this family. Make no mistake, Julian, this marriage is as much about her duty as yours."

Julian stiffened, his fingers tightening on the armrest. "Caroline is not some pawn to be manoeuvred, Father. She has proven capable of handling the ton's gossip with far more dignity than most."

"Capability is irrelevant," his father snapped back. "Her dowry and connections serve a purpose. The rest is immaterial."

"Immaterial?" Julian's voice sharpened. "You think it immaterial that she's intelligent, strong-willed, and willing to adapt to this family's rigid expectations? She might bring something more to this household than a title and fortune?"

The marquess's eyes narrowed. "Sentiment, Julian? I thought you better than that."

Julian leaned forward, his gaze unwavering. "Perhaps sentiment is exactly what this family needs. Have you considered that a home filled with warmth and genuine connection might serve our interests better than a cold, duty-driven façade?"

The tension in the room crackled like a live wire, the silence heavy and oppressive.

"Julian makes an excellent point." A smooth voice interrupted.

Both men turned to see Julian's elder brother leaning casually against the doorframe. Dressed impeccably, with his usual air of effortless charm, he stepped into the room, a sly smile on his lips.

"You're up early." Julian masked his surprise with a dry tone.

"How could I miss such a riveting debate?" The elder brother sauntered to the desk, pouring himself a glass of brandy as if it were midday. "Father, you should listen to Julian. Lady Caroline was the very picture of decorum last night. Poised, intelligent. Dare I say even captivating."

The marquess's expression darkened. "And what would you know of such matters, Thomas? You spend more time avoiding responsibility than embracing it."

Thomas raised his glass in a mock salute. "True enough. But even I can see that forcing this match without consideration for mutual respect and partnership would be a mistake."

"Partnership?" The marquess scoffed. "This is not a love match, Thomas."

"Perhaps not." Thomas flicked his gaze to Julian. "But it doesn't have to be loveless either. Give Julian some credit. He's not just doing this for the family, he sees something in her."

Julian shot his brother a sharp look, but Thomas only smirked.

"Enough." The marquess' tone cut through the room like a whip. "Julian, if you're so determined to make this work on your terms, then do so. But don't forget what's at stake."

"I never do." Julian rose slowly from his chair and grabbed his cane.

Julian and Thomas left the study together. In the hallway, Julian turned to his brother. "You surprised me in there."

Thomas chuckled. "Don't get used to it, little brother. But I meant what I said. She's good for you. It's good to see your permanent frown turned into a smile."

Julian frowned. "It's not that I don't smile."

"You always frown." Thomas clapped him on the shoulder. "Don't overthink it. Just don't let Father push her away before she's even had a chance to know you."

As Thomas strolled away, Julian stood alone in the vast, silent hall of Thornfield House. The emptiness pressed against him, a stark reminder of what he'd been raised to value—duty, legacy, appearances.

For the first time, he realised how much he wanted something different. Something warmer, something like the bustling, chaotic, and loving household in which Caroline had grown up.

With a resolute step, he started his journey to the stables to prepare for his trip to Osborne Hall. He had to make sure Caroline loved it as much as he did. He needed her. She would bring that warmth into his life and his home.

Chapter Twelve

Caroline and Julian rode side by side, the countryside unfurling in a vivid tapestry. They'd left before sunrise to allow the time it would take her to make the journey to Osborne Hall sidesaddle. She couldn't recall a time she had felt so alive. She was extremely excited to see her new home, to inspect the stables Julian had renovated for her horses and grooms, and to see Julian in his home environment.

The rhythmic sound of hooves on the packed dirt should have been soothing, but Caroline's heart was anything but calm. She would be meeting the staff today. Covered in dust and no doubt walking stiffly from holding her position for a few hours, she wouldn't look like a viscountess. What if the staff laughed at her? She shook herself free of the thoughts. It was too late to worry about that now.

She had never ridden into the countryside like this, and the journey was a revelation. Once they'd left London's pervasive odours and grime behind, she was entranced by the rolling fields, quaint villages, and the occasional glimpse of a stately home nestled amid lush greenery. She stole glances at Julian, his posture straight, his focus on the road ahead, his handsome profile etched against the clear blue sky.

Behind them, the carriage carrying Eleanor and their mother, Alexander, and Lady Beatrice rattled along steadily. Eleanor had insisted on the carriage, citing her delicate condition and the need to arrive without looking windblown. Lady Beatrice, never one to miss an opportunity for sharp commentary, had agreed, though not without pointing out that Caroline and Julian's choice to ride together was sure to fuel speculation among the ton.

"Better speculation than boredom," Caroline retorted, earning Julian a rare belly laugh.

Caroline suppressed a pang of guilt for leaving Eleanor to endure the company of Lady Beatrice's frank manner for hours. However, Alexander's steady presence and their mother's sweetness would temper the barbs. Hopefully.

"Are you holding up well?" Julian's deep voice cut through the peaceful silence.

Her face must've been glowing from exertion and exhilaration. Not at all viscountess-like, but again, she pushed the thoughts aside. "Perfectly, thank you. Are you worried I'll tire before we arrive?"

He gave her a quirky smile. "Merely ensuring you're comfortable. It's a longer ride than most might consider for a sidesaddle."

"I've ridden farther." She dismissed her comment with a wave of her hand. Though it was a minor exaggeration, her thighs and lower back were beginning to feel the strain of maintaining her balance for so long.

Julian's gaze flicked to her hands, no doubt noticing her deathly tight grip on the reins. "There's a charming inn about fifteen minutes ahead. It would not harm to pause for a brief rest."

"I'm perfectly capable of continuing—"

Julian raised an eyebrow, his expression equal parts challenge and amusement. "Humour me, Caroline."

She opened her mouth to retort, but the warmth in his eyes softened her resistance. With a sigh, she conceded. "Very well, but only for a moment."

The inn, a quaint structure with ivy creeping along its stone walls, appeared just as Julian had promised. He dismounted, and Brimstone patiently waited while he assisted Caroline. His hands lingered on her waist long enough to make her breath hitch, though his expression betrayed no more than polite concern.

Once her feet were on the ground, she stretched discreetly, grateful for the reprieve even as she pretended not to be. Julian led her toward a small bench beneath a towering oak tree. He fetched water for their horses, his limp pronounced, though his every movement remained efficient yet unhurried.

Caroline relaxed, and the cool shade was a welcome balm. "Do you often make this journey on horseback?"

Julian returned with huge glasses of ale for them both. "Whenever time allows. The countryside has a way of clearing one's mind."

She accepted the drink with a small smile. "I can see the appeal. It's rather freeing. Just you and the open road."

Julian's gaze lingered on her as he sat. "They do a decent lunch here, but Holly—Mrs. Hollybough—will have lunch ready for us. I will be in her bad books if we arrive full of someone else's cooking."

"From what you have told me of her, she sounds like a dear and a good cook. Hopefully she will forgive us." Caroline laughed at his perturbed expression. "This is surprisingly good ale. But I don't think the trip to Osborne Hall can go much further. Let's continue our journey."

"It's about an hour, I imagine." Julian checked his pocket watch. "We will have time to clean up and change before lunch." A quiet moment stretched between them, broken by the arrival of a stagecoach.

"It will be good to get out of these dusty clothes." Caroline brushed a stray hair from her face.

By mutual agreement, they continued their journey. When Osborne Hall finally came into view over the crest of a hill, Caroline drew in a sharp breath. The estate was magnificent. There was simply no other word for it.

Her heart swelled with apprehension. Osborne Hall was much more extensive and grander than she had imagined. Steeped in history. She tensed at the weight of it, not just as a future home but also as a responsibility. Could she genuinely belong here amidst such grandeur?

She tightened her fingers on the reins. With each step, the house loomed closer, its sheer scale intimidating. For all its beauty, it carried an air of solemnity, duty, and legacy that settled heavily in her chest.

"I told you it was magnificent." Julian's voice broke through her reverie. He watched her as she stared at his home, his expression softer than she had ever seen.

"It's... breathtaking." Her words faltered. "I don't know if I'm filled with admiration or overwhelming dread."

Julian's lips curved into a faint smile. "Both are appropriate. It has that effect."

"I'll find my place here. Somehow."

"You will, my love, of that I have no doubt."

Caroline's jaw dropped in surprise. "Oh... ah, you told me it was a sprawling estate, a hodgepodge of styles. You fibbed. "It's a vision from another time, a tapestry of English architectural history woven into one magnificent estate."

"One does not like to brag." Julian beamed at her. "The oldest section of the house is unmistakable, its Gothic origins evident in the steeply pitched rooflines, pointed arches, and narrow windows framed by timeworn stone."

Caroline slowed Silverthorne to a slow walk to take in more of the house while listening to Julian's proud baritone. Ivy crept across the grey walls, softening the edges with a romantic air. The very stonework of this part of the house seemed to whisper tales of centuries past.

"To the right, the Elizabethan wing rises in stark contrast." Julian gestured to the façade of warm red brick adorned with intricate mullioned windows and delicate stonework. "The gables are crowned with ornamental finials. Do you see the grand oriel window jutting proudly from the second story?"

"The glass panes are catching the late morning sunlight. It's beautiful, Julian."

"The Jacobean additions, though heavier in style, add an undeniable stateliness."

"I love how the decorated chimneys soar skyward like sentinels watching over the estate."

"You are very poetic this morning."

"Perhaps your home is inspiring me." Caroline gave a nervous laugh.

"Our home." Julian nudged her knee gently.

"Our home." She repeated the words, though she could hardly believe it.

Someone had added a sweeping colonnade to frame the central entrance, its clean lines and classical proportions orderly and refined. The stately symmetry of the Georgian style tempered the exuberance of the earlier periods, creating a harmonious blend that somehow felt inevitable, as though each era had been waiting for the next to complete it.

Yes, the house inspired her to poetic thoughts, but it was time to be serious. They had reached a fountain in the heart of a gravelled courtyard, its water sparkling like diamonds in the sun.

"It's even more beautiful than I imagined. Every single part of it." She swept her gaze across the symmetrical topiary and the vivid bursts of colour from neatly planted flower beds.

"Osborne Hall has been home to our family for generations." Julian's pride shone in his gaze. "I hope it will feel like home to you as well."

Caroline met his gaze, her chest tightening at the unexpected tenderness in his voice. "I'm sure it will."

Their arrival did not go unnoticed. As they dismounted, grooms ran to attend to the horses, and several staff members gathered at the entrance. Julian introduced her to the housekeeper, the butler and the cook. Nell had travelled ahead and stepped forward to take Caroline's saddle bag and discretely hand her a fan.

Julian gestured for Caroline to follow him inside. She stepped into the stone-flagged entrance hall and breathed a sigh of relief as she fanned her face. "The cool air is quite a relief."

"Let me show you to your room." Julian took her hand and guided her to the grand staircase. Nell darted ahead, her footsteps echoing in the vastness of the house. He checked his watch and lifted his brow in a question. "You have time to bathe if you choose."

"Both your housekeeper and I will appreciate it. I'm so dusty, I'm sure I would leave little piles of dirt wherever I sat."

Julian chuckled, brushing dust from his sleeve. "You are a little dusty, my dear, though I daresay I've fared worse. At the top of the stairs, he stopped. "I didn't want to incur the wrath of your relatives, so I've placed you with your family in the guest wing rather than in the room adjacent to mine, which is meant for the mistress of the house."

His cheeks reddened, a charming contrast to his usual composure.

Caroline grinned, tightness from the journey melting away. She poked a playful finger into his chest. "I understand. Probably for the best, but surely, as the future mistress of the house, I'm allowed a glimpse of my domain?"

His blush deepened, spreading to his ears. Adorable.

"I can permit that." He kissed the back of her hand and led her down a quiet hallway. He opened a polished door with a flourish.

The space was a vision of Regency elegance. Cream wainscoting framed pale green wallpaper, which contained a delicate floral pattern intertwined with gilded accents. A four-poster bed stood against one wall, draped with sheer curtains that pooled like clouds on the floor. Bright midday sun filtered through tall windows and cast a golden glow over a seating area arranged by a marble fireplace. Beyond the windows, the gardens stretched out in vivid greens and bursts of colour, and the topiary and flowerbeds she had admired earlier were now a breathtaking panorama.

Caroline's breath hitched. This was, without a doubt, the nicest bedroom she had ever seen. "This is my room?"

Julian lingered in the doorway, his gaze softening as he watched her take it in. "I had it redecorated. Do you approve? Of course, if you want to change anything—"

"It's perfect." She interrupted. Emotion welled in her chest. The enormity of this new chapter in her life was suddenly tangible.

He stepped closer, his presence steadying. Gently, he cupped her cheek, his touch warm against her skin. "You'll do wonderfully here, and I can't wait for us to wed."

Before she could respond, his lips brushed hers in a brief kiss, leaving her aching for more. He pulled back, his dark eyes holding hers. "I'll see you downstairs for lunch. Nell will show you to your room and help you get ready."

Caroline nodded as she swallowed the lump in her throat.

Moments later, Nell entered the room with an eager curtsy. "It's a right rabbit warren here, Miss—at least in the servant quarters and hallways. But I've already got my bearings."

Caroline smiled. Nell's enthusiasm was infectious. "Where have they put you, Nell?"

"In the guest room, I have a cot in the dressing room, but here." She gestured to a discreet door to the left. "I have a lovely small room of my own through that door." She dropped her voice to a conspiratorial whisper. "The master bedroom is through the door opposite."

Caroline's cheeks heated. No doubt she was as red as Julian had been moments earlier. "Come, let's go to my allocated room and get cleaned up."

The transition was smooth, Nell chattering about the servants and their tight lips as they made their way to the guest wing. Caroline didn't doubt for one moment that Nell would have them all eating from her palms before they had to return home.

The assigned guest room was lovely, with a canopied bed and tasteful furnishings, but it lacked the personal touches she had already begun imagining for her mistress' chambers.

A refreshing bath rejuvenated her, nerves soothed by lavender-scented water and one of Nell's magical neck massages.

Nell dressed her in a pale blue day dress scattered with delicate yellow flowers. The fabric was light and perfect for a sunny afternoon. As Nell fastened the final button, Caroline caught a glimpse of herself in the mirror. The journey's dust and fatigue had vanished, replaced by a calm exterior. But her heart still raced with anticipation about what the rest of the day would bring.

"Ready, miss?" Nell gave the ribbon under Caroline's bust one final adjustment.

Caroline smoothed her skirt and drew in a shaky breath. "I am as ready as one might hope."

Chapter Thirteen

The stillness of Osborne Hall often helped Julian calm his restless thoughts. But this morning, as he waited for Caroline to descend the grand staircase, the silence gnawed at his soul.

His mind was a whirlwind of thoughts. He kept asking himself the same question over and over. Should he tell her about his father's ultimatum? The estate he loved, the home that had become his sanctuary, hung in the balance. He'd never forget his father's expression as he held the two documents. One set cementing his ownership, the other giving his home to Robert.

He had less than six months to marry, or no doubt, his father would take great pleasure in tearing up the title deeds in his name in front of him. He couldn't lose it.

But, spirited, captivating, and trusting Caroline had agreed to marry him without knowing the whole truth.

He'd seen the cost of dishonesty in his parent's marriage. He didn't want it in his own. Honesty was a cornerstone of trust, whether leading men to battle or building a partnership based on respect. However, whenever he imagined the conversation, he saw their fragile warmth shattering.

Telling her could derail everything they'd built so far—the

friendship, the spark of mutual understanding that had begun to grow. Would she see him as a man who wanted her in his life, or as a desperate man clinging to his home in any way he could?

She might believe he didn't care for her at all. The thought of her smile fading, of her warmth turning cold, was unbearable. No. He couldn't tell her yet. Not when things were going so well.

He glanced up at the sound of her laughter. He'd recognise it anywhere—soft, vibrant, and unrestrained. The tightness in his chest eased when she appeared at the top of the staircase. Her smile brought sunlight into the shadows of his mind. Delicate curls framed her face, and though she must have been tired and stiff from her ride, she looked radiant.

Her maid, Nell, trailed behind her, carrying the lively energy of someone who adored her mistress. No surprise, given Caroline's openness and warmth with everyone regardless of station.

Julian pushed himself away from the wall, leaning slightly on his cane as he moved toward the staircase. Her sudden gasp of surprise startled him.

"You appeared so suddenly!" Laughter spilled over her words.

Julian chuckled, her mirth easing the knot in his chest. "I thought you saw me waiting for you."

The butler, alerted by her small shriek, approached with concern. Julian waved him off with a faint smile, his focus still on her.

"I must have been distracted." She rested an ungloved, delicate hand on the banister, shaking her head as she caught her breath. "Nell and I have been exploring and admiring the many portraits of your ancestors."

"Would you like a proper tour while we wait for the others to arrive?" He offered her his arm. "Nell as well, of course. We can't have you unchaperoned while waiting for your family."

Her face brightened, her enthusiasm intoxicating. "Oh, yes! I want to see everything. And I have questions."

"Questions?" He smirked. That playful glint in her eyes no doubt boded trouble. "Ask away, my dear. But don't be disappointed if I don't reveal all my secrets."

She laughed, swatting his arm lightly. "We will see about that."

"First question." She turned to him. "Forgive me if I'm being inexcusably nosy. This is a wonderful estate, and I am glad it is yours, but I wonder why it is yours and not your older brother's."

"That's easy to answer—this is the old Osborne Estate. My father decided it was too old, ugly, and cumbersome to renovate, so he moved his main residence to the larger estate and built a stately Georgian home. He now lives year-round in London at Thornfield House. Robert hates this place. He finds it too old and inconvenient for modern tastes and entertaining, so he resides at the newer estate. I, however, find its history grounding."

Her eyes softened as she studied him. "It suits you."

He nodded, caught off guard by the genuine affection in her tone. She meant it, not as a polite remark, but as a reflection of how she saw him. The thought warmed him in a way he hadn't expected.

He walked her through the two drawing rooms, one Georgian and the other decidedly older. She delighted in the music room and paused before portraits and tapestries, her questions tumbling out faster than he could answer. He withheld some of the house's quirks, Wanting to let her discover those alone. Surprises were part of the charm.

They stopped when they reached a portrait of his grandmother, Lady Rosamund Osborne, resplendent in crimson. "Your engagement ring originally belonged to her." His voice softened as he gestured to the sapphire on her finger in the painting.

Caroline studied the portrait for a long moment before murmuring, "She looks formidable."

"She was, but also full of warmth. She would've liked you."

The sound of carriage wheels crunching over gravel broke the moment. He sighed, and a flicker of tension returned. "Your family has arrived."

Caroline grinned. The love within her family was so important to her. It made him want to please the visitors. Please them to please her. Arm in arm, they stepped out to greet the newcomers.

Eleanor descended from the carriage with Alexander's help, her delicate condition obvious despite her radiant smile. "Well, this is positively charming." She swept her gaze across the grounds. "I imagine we'll all be quite comfortable."

Lady Beatrice and Lady Darrow followed.

Lady Beatrice swept a sharp gaze over the estate, her eyes narrowing as if appraising every brick and blade of grass. "Well." She laced her tone with theatrical scepticism. "It's larger than I anticipated." She sniffed, her expression hovering between disapproval and grudging acknowledgment. "But is this ostentation truly necessary? Especially in such a provincial backwater?"

Caroline bristled but kept her tone light. "I think it's rather magnificent, and the countryside is charming."

"Magnificent, yes." Lady Beatrice narrowed her gaze to a mass of ivy clinging to the stone walls. "That ivy looks like it's plotting a coup against the stonework. I imagine it requires a great deal of upkeep. I hope you're prepared, my dear."

Julian's jaw tightened. "Caroline is more than capable of handling the responsibility."

Lady Darrow chimed in, her tone soothing but heavy with concern. "It's a lot to manage, darling. Are you sure you are ready?"

Eleanor, ever the peacemaker, interjected with a laugh. "It's not as though she's running it alone. I have no doubt Julian's staff are up to the task, and Julian is invested in its care."

Julian nodded, his gaze steady on Caroline. "My staff is loyal and experienced. Caroline will have all the support she needs."

Alexander clapped him on the shoulder, his smile genuine. "We thank you for your generous hospitality, Julian. Perhaps we could be shown to our rooms to clean up before lunch?"

The tension eased slightly, though Julian couldn't shake the feeling that Lady Beatrice was cataloguing every flaw and shortcoming for later critique. As the footmen began unloading the carriage, Caroline turned to him, her expression determined despite the lingering shadow of her family's words.

"Thank you," she murmured. "For standing by me."

Julian met her gaze. "I always will."

She tried to hide her blush by quickly releasing his arm and turning to her family. "I will show you to your rooms. We are all together in the guest wing."

The foyer emptied. Julian stood still for several moments before striding to his study. He poured himself a large brandy. This wasn't the start of the visit he'd hoped for. He took a large sip of his drink and grinned at the empty room. Caroline had defended him and his home like a champion. And Alexander's touch had felt like solidarity. It was baby steps. But baby steps in the right direction.

Lunch was formal, served in a dining room that seemed almost too grand for the six of them.

Mrs. Hollybough had gone to great lengths to reflect the estate's prestige and showcase her kitchen skills. The table was laid with crisp white linens, polished silverware, and fine china imported from France many generations ago. A centrepiece of fresh flowers from the estate's gardens drew admiration from Caroline, Eleanor, and their mother.

Lady Beatrice, though, was determined to find fault. The perfume from the flowers was too strong. She found the white soup too thick, the poached salmon sliced too thin, and the lemon syllabub too tart. Through it all, Caroline batted away the criticisms and spoke glowingly about the home that would soon be hers.

He wasn't sorry when the older ladies retired to their rooms, and Alexander took Eleanor for a quiet stroll in the garden.

"Goodness." Caroline shook her head. "I'm sorry, Julian. They behaved like a pack of wolves circling their prey."

He had to agree, but he kept his tone light. "Lady Beatrice has a tongue on her."

"She does. I want to thank Mrs. Hollybough and the cook. Lunch was marvellous, and everything was delicious."

"She will appreciate hearing that from you, I'm sure."

Julian escorted Caroline to speak with Holly. Mrs. Hollybough was all brisk efficiency and clipped professionalism, and Caroline, while poised, seemed overwhelmed. When she desired to visit the kitchens and thank the staff, Mrs. Hollybough politely but firmly refused.

Caroline blinked fast, clearly taken aback by the rebuff.

Julian intervened. "Mrs. Hollybough, thank you. I'll take Lady Caroline on a tour of the stables."

Caroline turned to him, relief evident in her expression. "Thank you."

As they stepped into the fresh air, he caught her hand, his thumb brushing lightly over her knuckles. "Don't mind Holly. She's old-school. Ladies do not enter the lower realm in her world. You're doing well here, Caroline. You will have them all eating out of your hand in no time, just like Brimstone."

"I doubt that, Julian." She blew out a deep sigh before a radiant smile lit her face. "Brimstone is a lovely horse. Almost as nice as Silverthorne."

Thank goodness her cheek had returned. Julian chuckled. "We'll say hello to them both in a moment."

"Wait." Caroline pulled him back. "I need some carrots. But I can't very well waltz into the kitchen now—"

"No need." Julian tugged her back. "We will purloin a few from the root cellar."

With her pocket full of carrot pieces, they made their way to the two large paddocks that housed the old and newly renovated stables. The closer they stepped, the more Caroline's spirits improved. When Silverthorne and Brimstone came into view, peacefully grazing in adjoining paddocks, she sighed softly. "She's already settled in beautifully."

"She has. Just like you will."

Caroline didn't respond instead calling Silverthorne. The mare trotted over, Brimstone mirroring her movements. Both nosed Caroline's hands as they looked for the carrots. She stroked Silverthorne's neck, her earlier tension melting away.

"I hope so." She met his gaze with a soft smile. "Thank you for knowing exactly when I need a moment to breathe."

Julian's lips curved into a faint smile. "Always, Caroline."

She bounced on her toes. "This is so beautiful. Can I see her stall?"

"Of course." He led the way to the newly renovated stable block, trying to see the set-up through Caroline's eyes.

"Look at it." She squealed with delight as she danced around the central trough fountain in the cobbled courtyard. "It's the prettiest stable block I've ever seen."

The warm, weathered stone now had a newly slate tiled roof, and its large double doors, freshly painted forest green, stood open to welcome horses and visitors alike. Knowing how much Caroline liked garden spaces, he was glad he'd left the ivy climbing over the structure and the flower beds surrounding the building and courtyard.

"It has eight stalls, so you have room for another two horses. Any more than that, and we might have to negotiate." He lifted his brow.

"Julian, it's wonderful. I couldn't be more pleased."

"I haven't yet shown you the dedicated tack room, the wash stall, and the circular training yard."

She retook his arm. "Then what are we waiting for?"

They wandered through the stables and into the gardens. Osborne Hall would challenge her, he didn't doubt it. But if anyone could rise to the occasion, it was Caroline.

As the tour wound down, Julian led Caroline toward the library, his steps slowing as they approached the heavy oak doors. "This the heart of Osborne Hall. My heart, at least."

He pushed the doors open to reveal a room bathed in golden light. The late afternoon sun streamed through tall windows, casting a warm glow over the floor-to-ceiling bookshelves lining the walls. Leather-bound volumes filled the shelves, their spines a kaleidoscope of earthy hues. The air smelled of aged paper, book glue, and polished wood—oddly comforting and always grounding.

Caroline stepped inside, her gaze sweeping the room with wide-eyed wonder.

Nell tiptoed into the room and found a chair far enough away to give them privacy, close enough to give the illusion of a chaperone. She had been so quiet and unobtrusive the whole afternoon he'd forgotten she was even there.

Caroline darted to the closest bookshelf. "It's beautiful." She ran her fingers lightly over the spines of the books. "It feels almost alive, like an old friend."

His chest tightened at her words. She understood. "It's my sanctuary. When the world outside becomes too much, this is where I come to breathe."

She turned to him, her expression soft but searching. "Is it still too much? The world, I mean. For you?"

He hesitated. Why had he said anything at all? This wasn't something he felt comfortable talking about. But this was Caroline. His future wife. His fiancée. Absentmindedly, he brushed his fingers across the back of a nearby chair. "More often than I care to admit."

Caroline stepped closer. "You don't have to tell me, but if you ever want to, I'm a good listener..."

He exhaled slowly, the weight of her gaze comforting in a way he was not used to. Not yet, but—at a primal level—he was aware he yearned for it. He was at a crossroads. He could retreat into his usual silence or create a deflection. But how she looked at him—steady, patient, without judgment—made him want to share, even if only a little.

"The war..." His voice faltered, and he cleared his throat, his gaze fixed on the worn rug beneath their feet. "War changes a man. You think you know who you are, what you're capable of, but the reality..." He paused, searching for the words. "The war changed everything. It stripped me of who I thought I was and left pieces I'm still trying to put back together."

Caroline stepped closer and brushed her fingers along his sleeve. He almost felt the touch. "And yet you came through it," she said softly. "You're still standing."

"Some days, it feels like a hollow victory." He swallowed. Now that he'd started, he wanted to try and make her understand. He ached to have just one person who empathised with him. But that wouldn't be fair. He couldn't dump his baggage on her as if she were a convenient valet stand. He swallowed again, his throat thick. "The things I saw and had to do... they don't leave you. Will never leave me. The men in my care. Men who..."

He swallowed the hard lump in his throat as awful images assailed him. Men who perished quickly. Men who were viciously torn apart. Men who died slow and agonizing deaths. No. It would never leave him. There was much he would take to his grave.

She rested her hand lightly on his chest, her touch grounding. "You've endured more than anyone should have to. But you don't have to face it alone. Not anymore. I'm here now. I hope you'll let me help, even just by listening."

He looked at her then, honestly, and the walls he had so carefully constructed seemed to waver. "Thank you." His words carried more weight than he intended. "For being here. For not turning away."

Caroline's warm, unwavering smile filled his chest with warmth. "I wouldn't dream of it."

The room fell into a comfortable silence that didn't demand words. Julian led her to a chair near the hearth, gesturing for her to sit. He poured each of them wine from the sideboard, the deep crimson liquid catching the firelight as he handed her a glass.

"To new beginnings." He lifted his glass in a toast to her, his voice steady despite the emotions roiling beneath the surface.

"To finding our way." Caroline met his gaze.

They sipped in silence, the quiet crackle of the fire the only sound. For the first time in years, Julian felt something akin to peace—a fragile, tentative peace, but peace, nonetheless.

He watched Caroline, her lovely face lit by the fire's glow, and allowed himself a sliver of hope.

Perhaps, with Caroline by his side, he might finally begin to heal.

Chapter Fourteen

The soft clip of boots against stone echoed across the floor, drawing Julian's attention from the stack of ledgers spread across his desk. His mind had wondered anyway, to thoughts of Caroline—her warmth and wit, the way her eyes lit up when she was determined to prove her point. He glanced up with a smile on his face. But the interruption wasn't Caroline. His brother, Robert, strode into the study, his usual confident smirk firmly in place.

Julian set down the document he had been reading, his chest tightening with wariness. Robert rarely visited, never without contacting him first. "What brings you here?"

Robert spread his arms wide as if his arrival were the most natural thing in the world. "Good morning to you too. Can't a brother visit without suspicion? Half of London is abuzz with your engagement, and I can't answer their questions. I'm getting tired of my brooding mystery act. How do you keep it up so well?"

A bolt of lightning flashed bright light into the room, followed not many seconds later by a rumble of thunder.

Julian held back a sigh and called for coffee. Somehow, he kept dripping sarcasm from his words. "It helps if it's not an act."

Robert guffawed. His smirk softened as he sank into a chair. "She's visiting this weekend, isn't she? I'm a little disappointed you didn't extend an invitation to me."

Julian avoided his brother's gaze, shuffling papers unnecessarily. "Caroline is not yet up. But you are welcome to join me for breakfast."

"Don't mind if I do." Robert's smirk softened into something more thoughtful. "She's impressed you. That's rare, Julian."

Julian avoided his brother's gaze. "She's capable. Intelligent. And surprisingly perceptive."

Robert leaned forward, his tone losing its flippancy. "Good. You'll need someone like that to deal with Father's meddling."

Julian stiffened. "What do you mean?"

"Oh, come on, Julian. Do you think I don't know about the ultimatum? Marry in six months or lose the estate?" Robert's expression darkened. "Typical of him. It's so bloody dramatic. It's a damned unfair position he's put you in."

Julian's jaw clenched. "It's not something I've shared with Caroline. I've no intention of father's manipulation taint her view of this engagement."

"You may not have a choice. Servants are talking, and we both know gossip spreads like wildfire."

Julian's heart nearly seized. He'd always known that the marquess had placed loyalists among the staff at Osborne Hall. It was a calculated risk to leave them in place. Finch had identified them early on, and Julian reasoned it was safer to tolerate known spies than risk his father replacing them with someone far better at hiding their motivations.

Had the gamble unravelled?

He rolled his shoulders to try and ease the tautness there.

Nell was the kind of servant who wheedled information out of others and always let her mistress know. How much had she heard in the servants' hall?

Before Julian could respond, the door creaked open. Caroline stepped inside. Her gaze flicked between the brothers, her sharp eyes narrowing. "Secrets? Servants gossiping? Is there something I should know?"

Julian froze, but Robert, ever the opportunist, rose and gave an exaggerated bow. "Lady Caroline, it is a pleasure to see you again. Sadly, I must take my leave."

Robert turned to Julian and mouthed, *Best of luck.*

Robert's departure left an uncomfortable silence in his wake. Caroline crossed her arms, her voice low and measured. "What did he mean, Julian?"

Julian ran his hand through his hair. "It's not what you think—"

"Then explain," Caroline interrupted, her tone sharp. "What haven't you told me?"

He hesitated her gaze's weight and worry pressing down on him. "I've been meaning to tell you—"

"What secret? If you don't tell me right now, I will leave and never return."

The ultimatum hit him like a physical blow. Damn it. This isn't how he wanted her to find out. Apart from the truth, he couldn't think of anything that might satisfy her. "It's my father." He tried to let all his vulnerability show, but brick by brick, his walls were building back up. "He set an ultimatum—marry within six months, or Osborne Hall will pass to Robert."

Caroline's expression shifted from shock to disbelief to something that cut deeper. Hurt. "This engagement...was it ever about me? Or is it only about this estate?"

"No." Julian's frustration mounted. "Caroline, this is more complicated than you realise. I had no intention of rushing into anything, but then—"

"Then what? You decided I was convenient. Naïve enough to fool?" Her voice cracked, and the raw vulnerability in her tone sliced through him.

"That's not it." He stepped closer, but she took a step back. "This arrangement—our engagement—it's not just about the estate. I care about you."

"I trusted you, Julian, and you lied to me. I thought we were building something real, something honest." She shook her head, her composure faltering. "But you didn't trust me enough to tell me the truth."

Julian's face contorted with pain. "We were...we are building something real. My feelings for you are genuine, Caroline. Please believe me."

She backed away. "How can I believe anything you say now?"

"That was never my intention," Julian pleaded. "I feared if you knew, you'd feel trapped. That you'd resent—"

Without a word, she turned and fled, her skirts swishing as she raced through the corridors of Osborne Hall and slammed the side door on the way out.

"Caroline!" Cane forgotten, he limped after her.

"My lady!" Mrs. Hollybough's scandalised voice called after her, but Caroline paid no heed.

Pain flared in his leg, sharp and unrelenting. Gritting his teeth, he leaned against the wall.

"I'll send someone after her, sir." Holly turned to go and raise the alarm.

"No." Julian snapped. "I'll go after her."

"But, sir, your leg." Holly looked close to tears.

"To hell with my leg!" Julian immediately regretted his tone. He softened his voice. "Forgive me, Mrs. Hollybough. Please have dry clothes and hot tea ready for when we return."

"Colonel." Finch came running from somewhere and helped take his weight.

Julian leaned heavily on Finch's shoulder, every step sending a jagged pulse of pain through his leg. His frustration simmered just below the surface, threatening to boil over. Of all the times for this cursed leg to fail him, now—when Caroline hurt and furious, was running headlong into a storm—was the worst.

"Help me." Julian rasped through clenched teeth as Finch eased him into a chair in the study. "Camphorated oil and willow bark tea. And have Sam prepare Brimstone."

Finch hesitated for just a moment before giving a brisk nod. "Right away, Colonel." Finch disappeared with the efficiency Julian now relied on.

Julian rested his head against the chair's back, his breathing uneven. Somehow, he had to push through the pain. Thanks to him and the hurt he'd caused her, Caroline was in danger.

She had looked so betrayed. Her eyes, which usually sparkled with warmth and wit, had been filled with a hurt so deep it twisted something inside him. He'd wanted to tell her that his feelings for her had grown beyond the estate and its legacy. But the words had stuck in his throat, tangled in the weight of his pride and the fear of losing her. And then she'd left, not wanting to hear his excuses.

He couldn't blame her.

Finch returned swiftly with a small jar of camphorated oil and a steaming cup of tea. He helped Julian out of his britches and knelt to massage Julian's thigh, his hands deft and practised. The pungent aroma of the oil filled the room, mingling with the bitter scent of the tea.

"You'll find her, Colonel."

Julian sipped the foul-tasting astringent tea. He deserved the bitterness. "She's hurt and angry, and I pushed her to it."

He grunted as Finch used his thumbs on a deep knot of pain. He'd earned it. "Caroline deserves better than half-truths and ultimatums."

Finch paused, his hands stilling momentarily as if considering his words. "You will find Lady Caroline, sir. You will explain, and she will understand."

Julian managed a faint smile. "You have a way of putting things plainly, Finch. Too plainly, perhaps."

"It's a talent." Finch resumed the massage. "The tea should help ease the worst of it. And the oil will do its work. Give it a moment, and you'll be on your way."

Julian nodded, his resolve hardening. Finch was right—he wasn't a man who gave up, not on Osborne Hall, the legacy entrusted to him, and certainly not Caroline.

As the throbbing in his leg began to subside, Julian tested his weight, standing cautiously. The pain was still there but manageable now, a dull ache rather than a sharp stab. He retrieved his cane, gripping it tightly.

"Finch, if she hasn't taken Silverthorne, send someone to search the grounds."

Finch nodded and left to do his bidding.

But she was on her beloved horse. Of that, he was certain.

The stables were in chaos by the time Julian reached them. Silverthorne's stall was empty, and the stablemaster confirmed what Julian feared—Caroline had ridden alone, astride and saddleless on Silverthorne as dark clouds began to gather on the horizon.

A stable boy approached with a report. "She headed toward the woods."

Eleanor ran toward him. "What has happened, Julian? Is it Caroline?"

In silence, he debated what to tell her.

"Julian." Eleanor prodded him in the back. "I will get Alexander if you do not—"

"Are all the Darrow sisters so damn impertinent and independent?"

"Yes, so get used to it." Eleanor tapped her foot.

Julian sighed. This is what family meant, he reminded himself. People caring about one another. "I upset her. She ran to her horse and took off."

"Of course, she did." Eleanor blew out an annoyed sigh. "That's not abnormal for Caroline. She will come back when she's ready."

"There's a storm coming," Julian said, his tone clipped. "If she's caught in it—"

"Caroline knows how to handle herself on a horse," Eleanor interrupted, though her voice wavered. "If she's hurt, give her time."

Julian shook his head. "She doesn't know this estate. She especially doesn't know the woods or the weather we get here."

Brimstone was saddled and pawing the ground. Sam stood beside him with a block to help Julian mount. Ignoring the pain in his leg, he stepped into the saddle. "I'll find her." He gave Eleanor a nod.

A flash of lightning illuminated the courtyard followed by a deafening crack of thunder. Rain began to fall in heavy sheets.

In moments he was saturated, the wind tearing at his coat. He dug his heels into his horse's flanks, driving the animal forward into the deluge. The rain lashed against his face, each droplet feeling like a needle against his skin. He'd forgotten gloves, and his fingers were so cold it was difficult to hold the reins. His chest tightened at the thought of Caroline out there, angry and hurt.

"Caroline!" His voice was lost in the storm's fury. "Caroline, where are you?"

How could he have been so foolish? He should have told her the truth from the beginning. Now, because of his deception, she was in danger. The path into Blackwood Forest was treacherous in fair weather, nearly impassable in this storm. Julian leaned low over Brimstone's neck, pushing forward despite the branches that whipped at his face and arms.

"Please," he whispered to himself. "Please let me find before she is hurt or lost."

He pressed on, his leg throbbing mercilessly, but Julian pushed the pain aside, focused solely on finding Caroline before the storm worsened.

Brimstone hesitated at the edge of the dense woods, his ears flicking nervously. Julian dismounted, ignoring the protest of his leg, and led the horse forward.

Finally, beneath a cluster of trees, he spotted Silverthorne, her reins tangled in the branches. She whinnied softly, pawing at the ground. She was in distress, but she didn't seem otherwise hurt. Relief surged through him, but it was short-lived.

Caroline was nowhere in sight.

Chapter Fifteen

Caroline's heart pounded as she fled the suffocating confines of Osborne Hall. Her skirts swished in her agitation, the portraits of stern-faced ancestors silently judging her unladylike flight.

How could she breathe in that place? The air was too thick, too heavy with her family's expectations and his family's deceit. She fumbled with the side door latch, desperation lending her strength as she wrenched it open.

Cool, damp air hit her flushed face as she emerged into the gardens. Instead of soothing her soul, the manicured lawns and carefully tended flowerbeds felt like another cage. She spotted the stables in the distance.

"Silverthorne." She breathed the horse's name. With renewed purpose, she gathered her skirts and set off across the grounds, her pace quickening even as her house slippers slipped across the damp paving stones.

A stableboy squealed in surprise.

"Saddle Silverthorne for me. Hurry." Caroline's tone brooked no argument. She paced, fists clenched as the boy bridled Silverthorne and left to scour the stable, hopefully on a mission to find her sidesaddle.

He returned empty-handed. "I can't find ... Miss, are you sure? There's a storm coming—"

"I'm quite sure."

He wrung his hands in obvious distress, worry etched on his face. Caroline couldn't wait a moment longer. She grabbed a saddle blanket, draped it over Silverthorne and swung herself onto the horse's back with practised ease, propriety be damned. She urged the mare forward.

"I'll be fine," she called back. Though was it more to convince herself than him?

Exhilaration filled her as Silverthorne's hooves thundered across the grounds, carrying her towards the estate's boundaries and away from them—from him. Dark clouds looming on the horizon matched the tumult in her heart. She chose to ignore them.

Vaguely, she knew that she was endangering herself, but the thought of returning to Osborne Hall to face Julian, to confront the reality of her neatly arranged future, was unbearable. So, she rode on as the first fat, heavy drops of rain fell, the wind whipping her hair free of its pins.

Behind her, faint cries of alarm came from the household staff. As she reached the edge of the estate, the skies opened, and a cold torrent poured down, drenching her to the skin. But Caroline urged Silverthorne on, her only thought to distance herself from Julian's lies.

Thunder rolled, whether in ominous approval or warning, it was difficult to tell. Lightning flashed, illuminating her desperate flight.

Caroline ignored it all. The wind, the icy rain that stung her skin, the claps of thunder. She focused on the pain in her chest as piercing as the jagged bolts of lightning. She'd begun to trust him. How could he hide such a fundamental secret?

And yet, even now, she couldn't deny the pull he exerted on her heart. How could they have bonded in such a short amount of time?

A streak of lightning tore across the sky. A deafening crack of thunder followed, so close it rattled her bones. Silverthorne reared in terror, the horse's lithe body trembling beneath her.

"Easy, Silver, easy." Caroline's voice shook as she fought to steady her frightened mare, her ungloved hands slipping against the reins. Rain pelted down in relentless sheets, plastering her hair to her face. She squinted against the downpour, her vision blurred by water and tears she refused to acknowledge.

Her chest tightened with guilt. This wasn't just about her rashness now, Silverthorne was paying for her impulsiveness, her sides heaving with every laboured breath. What kind of mistress put her beloved horse in danger for the sake of her pride and fury?

A bad one, that's what kind. She had to slow down. Find shelter. Somewhere, anywhere to wait out the storm.

The thought barely formed before a jolt of terror sliced through her.

Silverthorne stumbled. Caroline hadn't noticed the fissure—dark and jagged like a scar across the earth—until Silverthorne's forelegs slipped into it.

"No!" The cry tore from her throat, raw and desperate.

Time slowed to a surreal crawl as Silverthorne twisted her body to try and recover.

The world tilted violently. The reins slipped from Caroline's grasp as she was thrown forward. Gravity pulled at her with merciless force, her body weightless one moment and hurtling over the mare's head next.

The ground rushed to meet her, and everything dissolved into a churning darkness.

She came to slowly, vaguely aware of pain and cold. A glacial cold that turned her insides to ice. A groan slipped from her lips. The wind seemed to scream her name. Great. Now, she was imagining things. Had she banged her head on a rock?

Silverthorne! Where was she? Dear Lord. Had she... Was Silverthorne okay? *Please, please* she implored the heavens. *Please let Silverthorne be okay.*

She couldn't hear the mare. Was it just because the sound of the storm drowned out most other sounds? She tried to lift her head to call her, but an agonising pain in her chest had her gasping and panting shallowly. Damn it, had she hurt a rib?

The sounds of a large animal lumbering through underbrush grew closer. She tried to lie completely still. Maybe it wouldn't notice her.

Then she heard it again, her name drifting on the wind. Had someone come to look for her?

"Caroline!" Julian grunted in pain. His voice cracked as he dropped to his knees beside her. "My God, Caroline, can you hear me?"

She fluttered her eyes open as he caressed her shoulder. "Julian?" His voice sounded small and far away. "Did you follow us?"

"As soon as I could. We need to get you out of this storm." He scanned her from head to toe as if assessing her condition and cataloguing her injuries. He pulled a flask from his pocket. "I had the forethought to bring brandy."

He opened the container and handed it to her. "It will help ease the pain of coldness."

The first swallow burned from her mouth to her stomach, and she tried to return the flask. But when the warmth started spreading outward from her abdomen, she clutched the flask to her chest.

She gripped his arm. "Silverthorne?"

"She's okay. She is covered in mud and her blanket was caught up in brambles and low branches, but she is otherwise okay. We will bring her with us."

Relief flooded her. The sensation was as relaxing as the warmth that followed the brandy.

"Just another few sips, my dear. I imagine you are unused to strong spirits."

She was, but she didn't care. If the brandy warmed her fingertips and toes, she would gladly drink the whole flask.

"If I lift you now, can you hold onto me?"

She nodded, determined to do her best if not for herself, then for Silverthorne, who needed shelter as much as she did.

"I'll have to get you onto Brimstone's back. He will have no trouble carrying both of us, and we can lead Silverthorne by her reins."

He lifted her to his chest. Even though he struggled to lift her onto Brimstone's back, he silenced her offer to help with a firm, "Let me take care of you."

She turned back to check Silverthorne for herself, but turning drew a squeak of pain from her. She sat with her back pressed against Julian's chest, his body warmth seeping through layers of wet fabric and into her skin.

An old stone folly came into view. It was built in a rustic cottage style, with a thatched roof and a wraparound-covered veranda. The horses could shelter from the rain there.

"Almost there." He grated out the words as if it were too difficult to talk through his pain.

Yet another consequence of her rashness. He'd come after her in this storm when he should have been home resting his leg.

Julian guided Brimstone through the gate, both horses onto the veranda, and dismounted. He helped Caroline down, his hands lingering on her waist to steady her and himself, perhaps. Try as she might, she could not hold in the gasp of pain from the movement.

Providence smiled upon them, and the door opened to Julian's touch. He turned to her. "Are you able to walk?"

She was about to say no when she noticed the pronounced limp and the taut lines of suffering etched across his face. She gave a resolute nod and hobbled inside. The small space was a little more spacious than her private dressing room. A large fireplace took up most of one wall, a modest closet stood opposite the door, and simple wooden benches lined each of the other weathered stone walls.

Julian started building a fire in the hearth. Still clutching the flask, Caroline settled on the bench opposite the fire. As the wood caught, flickering light cast wavering shadows across the room.

"I'm not fragile, Julian. You didn't have to come after me." Caroline murmured, unsure if he would even hear her above the sound of the storm. "But I am so glad you found me."

He turned to her, his gaze intense. "The thought of you alone, at the mercy of the elements... Do you imagine I could have remained idle, tortured by uncertainty over your fate?"

"I just needed space." Her voice wavered, betraying the tempest of emotions swirling beneath her composed exterior. "You didn't trust me enough to tell me the truth."

"I will not lose you." The raw vulnerability in his tone stripped away his usual aristocratic reserve. "The fear that if you knew, it would drive you away haunted my every moment."

"And deceit doesn't accomplish that same end?" Her eyes glistened with unshed tears, but her voice softened. "Julian, I need honesty. I need to know that I'm more than a means to an end."

"You are." He knelt before her, his hands resting on her knees with a reverence that spoke more eloquently than words. "You're everything I didn't know I needed. I'm terrified of losing you."

Her breath hitched, the vulnerability in his words disarming her. "You should have confided in me from the beginning."

"I know." He reached for her hand, his touch tentative. "I'll spend the rest of my life proving you can trust me. Will you let me see to your injuries?"

She nodded, then winced as he gently probed her ankle. "It's nothing, truly. Apart from the discomfort in my ribs, I'm more shaken than hurt."

Julian's brow furrowed with concern. "Nevertheless, we should bind it. Here—" He removed his cravat and used the damp silk to wrap her ankle with surprising tenderness and skill.

"You're shivering," She thrust the magical brandy into his hands.

"As are you." Julian managed a wry smile, but he accepted the offering and took a long swallow.

A charged silence fell between them, broken only by the storm's fury. Caroline dropped her gaze to her hands, twisting nervously in her lap. "Julian, I—I'm sorry for running away. It was foolish and reckless, and I've put us both in danger. Even worse, I could have caused Silverthorne—"

"No." Julian's voice cut through her self-recrimination with unexpected tenderness. He moved to sit beside her. "I'm the one who should apologise. I should have told you about my father's ultimatum from the beginning."

Caroline glanced up to study his face. "Why didn't you?"

He sighed, running his fingers through his rain-soaked hair. Oh, how vulnerable he looked at that moment. She wanted to accept his apology and kiss away all his worries. But she let him continue.

"I was afraid that if you knew the truth, you'd see our engagement as nothing more than a business arrangement. And I... I want it to be more than that. So much more. I believe, quite against all expectation, that I am utterly in love with you, Caroline."

"Oh, Julian." Caroline reached for his hand, needing his touch to ground her in this moment of raw confession. "Is that truly how you feel?"

Thunder rumbled, shaking the old folly's walls, and Caroline instinctively drew nearer to him. Their gazes met, and the air between them seemed to crackle with an energy that rivalled the storm outside.

"Caroline," Julian breathed her name like a prayer, his gaze flickering to her lips with unmistakable intent. Might I…"

"Yes?" She sank to her knees before him, propriety forgotten in the face of this greater truth.

Julian's hand trembled as he cupped her cheek.

No need for any more words, Caroline closed her eyes as Julian's mouth met hers. The first brush of his lips against hers carried all the tenderness of a question, but it quickly deepened into something more profound—an answer to longings neither had dared voice. The passion took her by surprise. Their lips danced in a frenzy of hunger and need, their tongues twining together in a desperate exploration. She gripped his shoulders and pulled him closer as the world seemed to fall away around them.

When they finally parted, both breathless, Julian traced the outline of her lips with his fingertip. "All I want to do is kiss you. But there is always a bloody chaperone around the corner."

"It won't always be this way." A soft laugh escaped her at the thought of any of her relatives waiting around corners in the hope of catching them en flagrante. "I was planning a swift wedding. Now I know about the ultimatum, we will make it as soon as possible."

His intense gaze met her own. "We are both thoroughly drenched." His voice was rougher than usual. "We should remove our sodden garments. Dry them by the fire."

Caroline's breath caught, and heat rose in her cheeks. Her simple day dress and shift, no match for the deluge, were plastered to her skin, revealing everything beneath. "Yes, I suppose we must."

She tried to reach the buttons at her back and gasped as a sharp pain sliced through her.

Julian hesitated, then gently took her hands in his. "Allow me."

Caroline's heart raced, but she turned so he could reach the buttons. He slid her hair over one shoulder and worked with deliberate care. Each brush of his fingers against her skin sent shivers through her that had nothing to do with the cold. The simple act of undressing was transformed into something far more intimate than she had ever experienced before, a surrender of sorts, though to what precisely, she could not yet name.

The crackling fire cast dancing shadows across the chamber as Julian divested her of her sodden dress. With trembling fingers, she reached for his waistcoat buttons, her movements hesitant yet determined.

Julian remained perfectly still, his breath quickening as she worked.

The mingled scent of woodsmoke and Julian's cologne—sandalwood and something indefinably masculine—created an intoxicating atmosphere in the small space. Caroline was dizzy with sensation.

"I've never…" The words caught in her throat as she met his gaze, and she could not express the magnitude of her inexperience. The confession lay unspoken yet perfectly understood.

Julian lifted his hand to cup her cheek. "Nor I. Not like this. Not with someone I…" His words trailed into silence, heavy with meaning.

Caroline leaned into his touch, her eyes searching his. "Julian," she breathed out his name. "I think I might be falling in love with you too."

The last barrier between them crumbled. Julian's lips met hers with a passion that took her breath away. Caroline melted into the kiss, her arms winding around his neck as she pressed closer. It was deep, breathless, a connection that spoke of longing.

They parted only when breathing became necessary, panting softly. Julian rested his forehead against hers. "Caroline," he whispered, his voice thick with emotion. "I never dared hope…"

"Nor did I." She traced the firm outline of his jaw, mapping the contours of this man who had somehow become essential to her happiness. "But now, I can't imagine any other path."

He kissed her cheek and rose with fluid grace. A cool draft sliced through her wet chemise, but he quickly found blankets in the closet and spread them on the rug in front of the fire.

He pulled off her chemise and immediately shielded her body with his own, wrapping a blanket around her shoulders. She gasped at the feel of skin against skin, a sensation both foreign and inexplicably right.

Julian's lips found hers again, this kiss deeper and more urgent than the last, as if some final barrier between them had dissolved in this moment of shared vulnerability.

Caroline responded with equal fervour, exploring the planes of his back, marvelling at the strength she felt beneath her fingertips. Strength previously only glimpsed through the precise tailoring of his coats.

When he laid her upon the rough blankets, it was with a reverence that pulled emotion from her very soul. Here, at this moment, stripped of all pretence and constraints, she glimpsed the true measure of his regard.

His dark curls, tousled by the storm and her fingertips, fell across his forehead in a way that spoke of transformation—the perfectly composed master of Osborne Hall giving way to simply Julian, a man whose fierce gaze held equal measures of desire and devotion. "I'm here." He pressed his lips to her temple with exquisite gentleness. "Always, I shall be here."

Caroline's fingers trembled as they traced the unfamiliar territory of his chest, noting how even her lightest touch could draw forth a sharp intake of breath. The differences between their forms fascinated her, his angles and planes so foreign to her own softer curves. Yet when his hands found her waist, drawing her closer, their bodies seemed to fit together with an inevitability that defied explanation.

"Are you certain?" Julian whispered, his voice husky with desire, tempered by evident concern for her well-being.

Was she? Maybe later she would think differently. But right at that moment, with the warmth of the fire at her back and the press of his skin against hers, she didn't want to be anywhere else. They were to be wed soon anyway. What did a few weeks earlier matter? Such distinction felt trivial against the profound rightness she felt.

Caroline met his gaze, and somehow, she kept her voice steady. "I've never been more certain of anything."

"You're trembling." Julian caressed her cheek tenderly.

Caroline smiled up at him, her fingers tangling in his hair. "It's not from cold anymore."

He gave her a slow, languid smile and withdrew from her embrace.

He stepped out of his breeches, and Caroline was captivated by the play of firelight across his form. She'd grown up on the Grantham Estate, she knew how animals coupled, and the maids' whispered confidences about marital relations had left her with clinical expectations. Still, nothing in their furtive conversations had prepared her for the profound intimacy of this moment. Nor for the size of ...

Indeed, nature could not intend... She drew back slightly, her eyes widening at this new understanding of what awaited them.

Julian gathered her close again, his kisses achingly tender, his hands moving with exquisite care across her skin. "Trust in me, my love," he murmured against her lips. "We are designed for this communion."

Trust. It all came down to that singular question. And yes, despite his earlier concealment and the circumstances that had led them here, she trusted him. Trust him to guard not merely her body but also the profound vulnerability of her heart.

Their bodies moved slowly, tentatively, and their hands explored each other's curves and angles. Their faces were flushed with desire, and in the flickering light, she had no doubt he could see the same raw emotion in her eyes as in his.

As her confidence grew, her explorations became bolder. She traced kisses down the column of his neck, savouring the slight salt of his skin. When she returned to claim his lips, she tasted a heady mixture of mint, brandy, and something uniquely, intoxicatingly Julian.

He traced the outline of her lips with devastating gentleness, each featherlight touch igniting tingles across her skin and sending shivers down her spine. This was Julian as she had never witnessed him, his customary reserve stripped away to reveal a passion that spoke to answering needs within her soul. Every caress seemed to carry profound meaning, and every shared breath was a silent vow between them.

As pleasure built like a rising tide, she clung to him, overwhelmed not merely by physical sensation but also by the intensity of emotion that threatened to consume her. The boundaries between them seemed to blur, each touch, each shared breath drawing them deeper into an intimacy that transcended mere physical union.

He pulled her nipple into his warm mouth. Warmth and wetness flooded her core, awakening something primal within her carefully composed nature. Her sex ached with the need for him to fill her.

Warmth pooled low in her belly, an ache building that spoke of needs she had never dared acknowledge in the light of day. Her body arched toward him of its own volition, seeking something beyond her understanding.

"Caroline," Julian breathed against her neck, his voice rough with desire. "Do you feel it? This connection between us?"

She could only nod, unable to form words as pleasure consumed her, her heart racing as she buried her face in the crook of his neck. She dug her nails into his back, wanting to leave a mark on this man who had captured her heart.

"Julian," she gasped out. She was falling deeper and deeper into him. In this intimate moment, she'd discovered a deep connection she never knew existed between them.

Afterwards, they lay entwined before the crackling hearth, Julian's arms wrapped protectively around her. She traced idle patterns on his chest, still marvelling at their intimacy. The firelight cast soft shadows across their skin, lending an almost dreamlike quality to their sanctuary.

"What are you thinking?" Julian asked softly, his fingers weaving patterns through her golden hair.

Caroline turned to meet his gaze with newfound confidence. "I'm thinking about how different this is from what I imagined when we first met," she admitted. "An arranged match, thrust upon us both. And now—"

Julian brushed his thumb across her lower lip. "And now?" he prompted, a hint of vulnerability in his eyes.

"Now, I can't imagine my life without you." Caroline leaned in to press a soft kiss to his lips. "What began as duty has become everything."

She nestled against his chest again, feeling safer and more content than she had in months.

"What happens now?" With a soft touch, she traced abstract patterns on his bare arm.

Julian pressed his lips to her temple. "Now, my dear, we face whatever comes together. No more secrets, no more doubts between us."

As the storm subsided, they sat entwined. Caroline felt a profound shift within her soul, as if the tempest had washed away her fears and hesitations, leaving her with a new sense of purpose and belonging.

"I believe." She glanced at Julian. "This may be the beginning of something truly wonderful."

Julian's answering smile was as radiant as the summer sun after rain. "Indeed, my love. The beginning of our future, forged in truth and trust at last."

In the gentle aftermath of their passion, Caroline reflected upon fate's curious workings. How strange that it had taken a storm's fury to strip away the carefully maintained facades they both had worn, revealing the deeper currents that had always flowed beneath the surface of their arranged match. Their union, conceived in calculation and necessity, had transformed into something far more profound—a love story written not in the pages of a novel but in the secret language of hearts finally laid bare.

Chapter Sixteen

It was the second day after the storm. Julian stood still for Finch to finish tying his cravat.

"Did you ever think we'd be in this position—warm, overly fed, constricted by fussy neckwear—when we were knee-deep in mud and gore on the battlefield, Finch?"

"It didn't occur to me that I'd get home at all, Colonel. Every day, finding your boots and tying your cravat is a bonus as far as I'm concerned." Finch grinned cheerfully. "Now, the carriage is ready as instructed, and Lord Weston and Lady Caroline await you in the breakfast room."

Finch's cheerful outlook on life snapped Julian from his memories. "Best not keep them waiting then."

Julian had to lean heavily on his cane as he made his way to the breakfast room as stiff as a string puppet. His leg protested every jarring step downstairs, but he refused to let it slow him down.

Inside, voices filtered through the doorway, rising in a heated argument. Julian paused for a moment before stepping in.

"Caroline is very sensible, darling." Eleanor interrupted Alexander before he could continue his lecture. "If she says she can manage the outing, then I'm sure she can."

"I rested all day yesterday as the doctor ordered." Caroline's cheeks sported adorable red spots, but she kept her voice even. "Nell has bound up my ankle and my ribs so tightly I can't imagine any harm coming to them even if I fall from the carriage."

"Good Lord, woman." Alexander tossed his napkin on the table, exasperation etched into his features. "Do not tempt fate." He turned to Eleanor, his voice softening. "Unlike your sister, please do as I say, not the exact opposite."

"I promise I will rest in the drawing room with nothing more strenuous than my needlepoint." Eleanor gave him a serene smile.

Caroline spotted Julian in the doorway. Her gaze brightened, and her smile tugged at something deep in his chest, a warmth he had almost forgotten existed.

They hadn't had a moment alone since he brought her back from the folly. Every glance and fleeting touch since had carried an unspoken understanding, a reminder of the intimacy they'd shared.

But, after *The Folly Incident*, as Lady Beatrice had so dramatically titled it, he couldn't imagine the Weston family permitting them to spend time together until the marriage licence was obtained, the church organised, and the invitations sent.

Caroline's version of how they spent the time until the storm eased enough for them to return was as pure as newly fallen snow. But Lady Beatrice was still appalled and insisted he get the marriage license immediately, lest gossiping servants spread the story far and wide.

"Are you going to argue with me also, Julian?" Caroline tilted her chin defiantly, her eyes sparkling despite the slight shadows beneath them.

"I wouldn't dream of it." He stepped into the room. "I agree with Eleanor."

Her deepened smile made Alexander's obvious annoyance worth it.

"My steward is expecting us, and the carriage is ready. Shall we?"

Caroline took his arm. She was still limping and breathing rather shallowly, but she was so pleased to be visiting the village on his estate that her enthusiasm was infectious. He had no intention of dampening it, he just had to make sure she came to no harm.

The morning air was sharp and fresh, but dampness lingered even though the river had mostly returned to its banks. Julian helped Caroline out of the carriage and offered her his arm to tiptoe across the muddy, rutted road.

Trees were down, numerous roof tiles lay in the road, and a muddy line showed the depth to which the water had risen. Caroline swivelled to inspect the damage to numerous village buildings but said nothing. She hesitated slightly before climbing a few steps, and a wince flickered across her face. His concern deepened.

"Your ankle?" he asked quietly.

"Just a little tender." She kept her focus on the village. "It's nothing compared to the trail of destruction I see before me."

Julian frowned. "It's more than a nothing. You really shouldn't be walking on it."

"I'm fine, Julian." The slight hitch in her step betrayed that she was far from fine. "It's just a bit stiff."

Alexander strolled on Caroline's other side, his protective instincts subtly evident. "I agree with Julian, Caroline. You need to rest. There's no need for you to join this inspection."

Caroline's mouth tightened, her chin lifting in quiet defiance. "I'm not about to sit idle while there's work to be done. Julian's steward reported that the village school is so badly damaged, the children won't be able to do their lessons, and an education is so important."

Alexander muttered something that sounded suspiciously like "stubborn Darrow women."

Julian suppressed a smile. Yes, he was worried about her, but her determination was one of the many things he admired most about her.

The walk was slow, owing to Caroline's sore ankle and Julian's aching leg. Each step sent a dull throb radiating from his thigh, but he set his jaw against the pain. He had endured far worse and would not let it slow him now.

"How is your leg holding up?" Caroline glanced at him with genuine concern.

"It's fine."

Her eyebrow arched. "That's not what Finch said this morning."

Julian shot a glare over his shoulder at Finch, who shrugged unapologetically. "It's manageable." He softened his tone. "But this isn't about me."

"It is if you collapse halfway there." She patted his arm. "The poor villagers will have to pick you out of the mud. We make quite the pair, don't we? Hobbling along like invalids."

Julian's lips quirked despite himself. "Perhaps we should have taken the carriage to the school."

Caroline's laugh was light, but it quickly dissolved into a wince as she inhaled too sharply. "I'm fine," she ground out before either man could speak, her voice firm. "Truly. Besides, the carriage would not have made it through these ruts. Better a sore ankle than risk the horses."

Julian exchanged a look with Alexander, who sighed heavily but said no more. Finch coughed discreetly behind them, likely stifling his own opinion.

"Are you quite sure the school is beyond salvage for now?" Caroline's eyes held an intensity that Julian was beginning to associate with her sharp mind.

"I trust my steward. If he says it could take months to repair, then I believe him."

Caroline's brow furrowed. "Months without lessons could mean years of setbacks for the children. That hardly seems acceptable."

Julian's lips quirked in a faint smile. "I didn't expect you to accept it."

She tilted her head, her eyes sparkling with the beginnings of a smile. "You know me so well."

Finch coughed discreetly behind them. Alexander, ever the perceptive brother-in-law, raised an eyebrow but said nothing.

"The school is the heart of this part of the estate." Julian gestured ahead. The small stone building sat at the edge of the village green, its windows dark and its yard eerily quiet. "When my grandfather built it, he said educating the next generation was as much a duty as cultivating the land. My father..." Julian's voice tightened. "He didn't share the sentiment."

Caroline glanced at him, her voice softening. "Neither did mine. For all his titles and estates, he thought education a frivolity for anyone who wasn't destined for Parliament or the clergy."

Julian's steps slowed as they approached the building. "It's not a frivolity. Educated tenants mean a stronger estate and better lives for their children. It's practical, if nothing else."

Caroline smiled, her expression thoughtful. "It's also compassionate."

By the time they reached the school, Julian's leg felt like it was on fire, but he pushed the discomfort aside as he took in the scene before him. When the river rose, thanks to the deluge, the school was the first to flood and the last the water receded from.

The storm had left its mark—multiple roof tiles were missing, windows were broken, and the ground around the foundation was sodden and uneven.

"Let's not linger," Julian said. "Caroline, if you're feeling—"

"Julian, for the last time, I'm fine. I see the schoolmaster and schoolmistress waiting for us near the entrance. Goodness me, the door is completely off its hinges. No wonder they look so worried. Let's continue."

Mrs. Pettigrew, the schoolmistress, and Mr. Harding, the schoolmaster, stood a little apart. Both looked equally worried yet relieved at the sight of them. His steward stood, arms crossed in front of them.

"Lord Osborne." Mr. Harding bowed. "The storm has left us in quite the predicament. We've salvaged some materials, but the damage is extensive."

Caroline winced sympathetically, her hand tightening on Julian's arm. "It looks terrible. What is the worst damage?"

Caroline tiptoed to the broken door, Julian following close behind. They stepped into the schoolhouse, the scent of damp wood and sodden paper hanging heavy in the air. A stack of books sat ruined in the corner, their spines warped beyond recognition. Chairs and desks were overturned, many damaged, and most still sodden from the floodwaters.

"Goodness me." Caroline gazed up at the ceiling. "That looks like a bad leak."

"The roof is badly damaged, my lady." Mrs. Pettigrew gave Caroline a stiff curtsy. "It's still leaking even though the rain stopped. The floors are waterlogged, and even the walls have loose patches."

Julian nodded. "Steward, you've inspected the damage?"

"I have, sir. Mr. Harding is correct. The damage is so extensive, it might be cheaper to pull this old building down and rebuild a new one.

"It's clear the school can't be used until it's safe, even if it can be repaired." Julian glanced at his steward. "Have a few alternatives to me by the end of the week if you can. If we can't repair, we will rebuild."

Mr. Harding wrung his hands. "The children will fall behind if left without lessons for too long."

Caroline's expression brightened. "What about Osborne Hall? It's not too far away. There's an unused wing, isn't there? The east wing, I believe. Couldn't we hold lessons there for now?"

He felt like hugging her, not that he would in such a public setting. Her compassion knew no bounds. But could it work? The suggestion hung in the air, and Julian felt pride at her quick thinking. "It's not ideal." He tapped his chin. "But it's spacious and dry. Finch, have the east wing prepared for temporary use. Desks, chairs—whatever they need."

Finch inclined his head. "Right away, Colonel."

Mr Harding's eyes widened in gratitude. "That's more than we could have hoped for, My Lord. Thank you."

Mrs. Pettigrew nodded fervently. "We'll ensure the children are well-behaved and respectful in the house."

Julian waved away their thanks. "The priority is the children's education. Let's make it work."

Julian escorted Caroline out of the building as the school staff discussed logistics with Finch. "You've just volunteered yourself to oversee this operation."

She laughed, and the sound was light and teasing. "It will be my honour. It's a worthy cause, and I enjoy a good project."

Alexander cleared his throat pointedly. "It's a fine idea, Caroline, but you've yet to set a wedding date. You can hardly oversee the project from London. Do remember to pace yourself. Nobody wants you falling ill from overexertion."

Julian hid a smirk. "I'll ensure she doesn't overdo it."

Caroline arched an eyebrow at him. "Will you, now?"

He leaned closer, his voice low enough for only her to hear. "You've proven you can be quite... persistent when you want something."

Her lips twitched, her gaze forward, but her expression unmistakably pleased. "I prefer the term determined."

"I've noticed." Julian softened his tone. "I rather enjoy it."

Their steps slowed briefly as Caroline glanced up at him, her eyes meeting his with an intensity that stole his breath. For a moment, the storm, the injuries, the lingering pain—all of it faded, leaving only her.

Alexander gave a slight cough and drew closer. "What are you two whispering about?"

"Just discussing the merits of cooperation," Julian said smoothly, though the look he exchanged with Caroline spoke of far more than logistical arrangements.

Alexander looked suspicious but let the matter drop as Finch returned to their side.

"A group of tenants has gathered, Colonel," Finch whispered.

Julian refocused on the school. A dozen people had gathered, many coated in grime and exhaustion. A few children peeked out from behind their parents' legs, and their wide eyes settled on Caroline, an unfamiliar sight.

He nodded and exchanged nods and brief greetings with the tenants. He needed to reassure them and help settle their anxiety. "We'll see the school rebuilt. And let my steward know of any other extensive damage we can help with."

One of the older tenants, a stout man with a weathered face, tipped his hat. "Thank ye, my lord. It means the world to us, it does."

Caroline stepped forward, her voice clear and warm. "And the children will have lessons in the east wing of Osborne Hall until the school building is safe. They mustn't lose any more time than necessary."

A murmur of surprise rippled through the small crowd, followed by smiles and nods of approval. As they glanced at Caroline, Julian saw admiration in several of their eyes, and a swell of pride rose in his chest.

Julian's leg protested with every step back to the carriage, but he barely noticed. His thoughts lingered on Caroline and how her presence breathed new life into his estate.

"You were remarkable today." Julian took advantage of Alexander moving momentarily out of earshot.

She glanced at him, her expression softening. "We make a good team."

Julian's chest tightened at her words, their simplicity striking a chord he hadn't known was there. Julian couldn't help but feel a swell of gratitude, not just for how Caroline had stepped in to address the school's plight, but for how she seemed to breathe life into everything she touched.

"Yes," he agreed finally. "We do."

She had brought warmth to his estate, determination to his tenants, and a spark of hope to his guarded heart. And in that moment, Julian knew he would do whatever it took to keep her by his side, not just as the future Viscountess, but as his partner in every sense of the word.

Chapter Seventeen

The drawing room of the Weston Townhouse hummed with lively chatter, the energy almost as chaotic as the stacks of fabric swatches and floral sketches spread across every available surface. Sunlight poured in through the tall windows, but the warmth in the air came entirely from its occupants.

Caroline sat at the centre of it all, her brow furrowed as she stroked her fingers across the delicate texture of two ivory silks.

"This one has a finer weave." Eleanor paused in her stitching, a serene smile lighting her face. "They will both make a lovely veil. But if you don't decide soon, you will walk down the aisle in a sunbonnet."

"Would that be so awful?" Olivia fanned herself as she sprawled inelegantly on a chaise. "Honestly, Caroline." She adjusted the pillows behind her back. "I'd forgotten how exhausting it is to be in a delicate condition. There is nothing delicate about it, I can tell you. Why didn't you plan your wedding for next spring? By then, I could have already been through my confinement and well on my way to recovery."

"Please." Eleanor blew out a breath. "You are not even showing yet. I, however, need more fabric than the modiste had in stock to disguise this spreading girth."

Caroline smirked, tapping a pencil against her chin as she reviewed the latest guest list. She would never tell anyone the reason for her haste in planning the wedding, but she voiced another, equally valid. "Because then Mary would have been halfway to Madagascar to document some rare flowers and would have been unavailable to attend."

Mary, her skin tanned to an unfashionable warm bronze from her latest tropical expedition, glanced up from the sketchbook she was flipping through with a laugh. "I'd have found a way to come back for you. But I'm glad you didn't wait. I wouldn't miss seeing you walk down the aisle for anything."

"It is a shame Alice will miss the wedding." Eleanor pausing mid-stitch. "She would have loved to help you with all the details."

"Good heavens, I would have been halfway to my dotage if we'd let Alice loose on the fine details." Caroline grinned back at Eleanor. "She's busy honeymooning in Europe. Having the time of her life and hardly sparing a thought for us."

Lady Beatrice sniffed from her chair near the fireplace, surveying the scene with the air of a seasoned general inspecting her troops. She tapped her fan thoughtfully against her knee. "Alice will return from her honeymoon brimming with opinions about how much better everything is on the Continent. Though I imagine she'll be too busy shopping for Venetian glassware to notice our humble efforts here."

Caroline bit back a smile and refused to rise to the bait.

"But what's this I hear about your honeymoon plans, Caroline?" Lady Beatrice continued, fixing her with a hawk-like gaze. "Spending it at Osborne Hall, overseeing the rebuilding of a school for tenants? My dear, I don't know whether to applaud you or have you committed."

Caroline lifted her chin, ignoring the pointed sarcasm. "Yes, that is my intention. The school is important, and I'd like to see the project off to a good start. Besides, Osborne Hall is home. Why would I want to be anywhere else?"

Lady Beatrice lifted her brow, her expression caught between disbelief and amusement. "Because it is what newlyweds do, my dear. Travel. Relax. Lie about in decadent accommodations with servants attending to their every wish." She fluttered her fan with mock drama. "Surely you don't plan to spend your honeymoon with a hammer and a pile of bricks."

"Some newlyweds do enjoy travelling far and wide." Caroline glanced at her sisters as she smiled sweetly. "I'm looking forward to tackling a pile of bricks with a hammer."

Mary stifled a laugh behind her hand while Olivia chuckled outright. "She has you there, Lady Beatrice."

Lady Beatrice sniffed again but didn't appear offended. "I'm quite used to being outnumbered by Darrow women, thank you. Though I am not used to this predilection for rural pursuits."

Lady Darrow, seated quietly by the window, spoke up, her voice gentle but with a wry edge, "I think it's admirable, Beatrice. Not every woman prioritises her tenants' well-being. Caroline has always been practical and forward-thinking."

"Thank you, Mama." Caroline's chest filled with warmth. It wasn't often she received such praise from her mother.

"Practical?" Lady Beatrice tilted her head, her sharp eyes glittering. "I suppose that's one way to describe the Darrow sisters." She paused, then added with a sly smile, "I must admit, it's refreshing to see at least one of you marry a man who isn't gallivanting off to the tropics or dragging his wife in a delicate condition across half of England."

Mary laughed. "I'll take that as a compliment, Lady Beatrice."

Olivia sat up slightly, fanning herself as she groaned. "I can't decide if she's scolding or praising us."

"Both." Eleanor chuckled. "Lady Beatrice can do both at the same time."

Lady Beatrice gave a small, satisfied smile and reached for her tea. "I do have a talent for multitasking."

Caroline's attention was stolen by the florist's sketch of cascading roses and lilies intended for the altar. Her heart raced with anticipation. This wedding was everything she wanted—intimate, meaningful, and hers.

She gripped the sketch and chose her words carefully. "Alice's wedding to Lord Lyndon was beautiful, but Osborne Hall feels right for Julian and me. It's where we'll make our home."

Their home. Joy bubbled to the surface, and words gushed out. "St. Mary's Chapel in the market town nearby is delightful, Lady Beatrice. It's a Norman-era stone church nestled at the edge of Alton. It's so serene. It's the perfect place for a quiet, intimate wedding steeped in history and love."

"Delightful." Lady Beatrice snapped her fan. "If anyone can make something provincial seem fashionable, it would be you and your sisters."

Ever the peacemaker, Eleanor looked up from her stitching with a soft smile. "Osborne Hall is charming, Lady Beatrice. And I found the town of Alton rather enchanting."

"It's not about grandeur." Caroline sent Eleanor a grateful glance, taking heart from her sister's support. "I want a day that's full of love, not spectacle. Something intimate and meaningful."

Her mind drifted, unbidden, to that stormy day at Osborne Hall and Julian's touch. His low voice, his steady hands. Heat flushed her cheeks at the memory, and she quickly bent over the florist's sketch to hide it.

"Are you feeling faint, my dear?" Lady Beatrice's sharp voice cut through her reverie. Her narrowed eyes gleamed with suspicion. "You've gone rather pink."

"Quite well." Caroline willed the blush to fade. "Just thinking of the floral decorations."

"Hmm." Lady Beatrice's gaze lingered before she picked up her tea again. "I hope you're not planning anything too modern. The last thing Osborne Hall needs is to be overshadowed by avant-garde florals."

The butler entered the room, his deep voice saving Caroline from further scrutiny. "Viscount Osborne."

Caroline snapped her head up, and her heart leapt at the sight of Julian in the doorway. His broad shoulders filled the frame, and his dark eyes swept over the chaos with a faint smile.

"Are you holding your own, my love?" he asked, his voice warm and teasing.

Caroline's heart swelled at the endearment, the words settling over her like a soft blanket. "Quite well, thank you."

Julian crossed the room to her, his movements as steady and purposeful as always. He bent to kiss her cheek, his lips lingering just a moment too long. Lady Beatrice gave an audible huff of disapproval, which they both pointedly ignored.

He sat close enough to Caroline that it took all her self-control not to rub against him like a cat. They chatted about inconsequential things until the butler tapped on the door.

He entered with a silver tray in hand. "A message for Lady Caroline."

Caroline took the envelope, the room momentarily quieting as she broke the seal. Her brows furrowed as she read the contents. "It's from the marquess. He's requested a meeting with me. Just me."

The atmosphere in the drawing room shifted. Eleanor remained still in her chair, Olivia sat upright, and Mary's expression became sharp.

Julian's eyes narrowed as he reached for the letter. He scanned it, his jaw tightening. "How dare he."

Caroline blinked at the force in his voice. "Julian—"

"No." He cut her off, his tone clipped but protective. "He has no right to summon you alone. You're my fiancée, not his to command."

Lady Beatrice leaned forward, her sharp gaze glittering with interest. "I assume, Julian, that you intend to address this?"

"Of course." He folded the letter neatly, his expression like stone. "I'll accompany Caroline. Whatever my father wishes can be said in front of us together."

"You'd defy the marquess openly?" Lady Beatrice's tone was almost impressed.

"For Caroline?" Julian's voice softened as he turned back to her. "Without question."

Caroline, her heart pounding, reached for his hand. "Thank you, Julian. But let's not let his command overshadow our joy."

The Thornfield drawing room was oppressively ornate, its gilded mirrors and heavy drapes smothering the light that tried to filter through the tall windows. Caroline sat stiffly on the edge of her chair, the marquess's sharp, calculating gaze cutting through her composure.

"You must understand, Lady Caroline." His tone was oily with condescension as if she should be fawningly grateful for his attention. "A viscountess must maintain the decorum of the family. Julian has always been too indulgent. It's time he learned the value of control—over himself and his household."

Caroline's jaw tightened, her instinct to retort stifled. She summoned a polite smile and masked her simmering irritation. How dare he? The man spoke as if Julian were nothing but an errant schoolboy. The sting of his words wasn't just directed at Julian, they were aimed at her, too, implying her inadequacy before she'd even had a chance to prove herself.

She forced her voice to remain even and thanked the heavens that they'd planned this subterfuge last evening. Julian had snuck in the back door and wasn't far away. "Julian and I share a mutual respect, my lord. I have no doubt we'll navigate our roles together successfully."

"Mutual respect." The marquess arched his brow, his smirk patronising. "Obedience is all that matters."

The door opened, cutting him off mid-sentence. Caroline turned and relief flooded her at the sight of Julian. He entered the room, his presence commanding and a balm against her nerves.

"I wasn't aware this meeting was taking place." He strode to her side, his hand brushing lightly against her shoulder as he sat beside her. His body radiated with controlled fury, his acting skills impressive.

The marquess's expression soured. "This is a private discussion."

"Anything concerning my wife concerns me," Julian replied. "What are you discussing?"

Caroline smiled at his deliberate use of the word "wife."

The marquess's lips thinned. "Merely offering Lady Caroline guidance on her future responsibilities."

Julian's gaze hardened. "Caroline is more than capable of determining her course."

Caroline reached for his hand and squeezed lightly. The marquess' disapproving gaze flicked to their joined hands, and her temper flared. Did he think she could not be her own person and stand at Julian's side?

"Sentimentality, Julian." The marquess sneered. "Will get you nowhere. It's exactly this sort of indulgence I was referring to. A man must rule his household with authority, not affection."

A visceral rush of anger filled Caroline. He'd raised his children with cruelty and now was intent on applying the same methods to her. How could anyone mistake care and respect for weakness? It didn't make any sense to her. But she could not interrupt. Julian had to face his father.

Julian's grip on Caroline's hand tightened briefly before he released it and leaned back, his gaze cool but sharp. "I see. And is that how you ruled yours, Father? With an iron hand and no room for compromise?"

The marquess bristled, the muscles in his jaw tightening. "Do not take that tone with me, boy. Everything I have done has been for this family—ensuring its name, legacy, and fortune endure. You would do well to remember the sacrifices I made for you to sit where you are now."

Caroline's stomach churned as she watched the tension build. Her heart ached at the weight Julian carried. He had endured this his entire life. This overbearing shadow that sought to control his every move.

Julian leaned forward slightly, his voice calm but laden with authority. "The legacy you speak of is not built solely on power or wealth. It is built on the respect and loyalty of the people who depend on us—our tenants, staff, and family. If you cannot see that, then perhaps it's you who needs reminding."

The marquess' eyes narrowed even further. "Do not presume to lecture me, Julian. You exist to serve the family and its interests. That includes obeying my will."

Caroline's breath caught, her chest unbearably tight. She could almost feel Julian's raw anger bristling just below the surface. He wouldn't back down this time.

Julian's jaw clenched. "Your will, Father, has interfered with my life for the last time. You've dictated the terms of my inheritance and my marriage, and now you presume to dictate the nature of my relationship with my wife. I won't stand for it."

The marquess rose to his feet, his voice cold and cutting. "Then perhaps you should reconsider whether you are fit to bear the Osborne name, let alone manage one of its estates."

Julian also stood, his height and controlled presence matching his father's oppressive energy. "You've made that abundantly clear, haven't you? Your ultimatum, your spies at Osborne Hall—I've tolerated it all out of respect for the title and the family name. But no more. Caroline is to be my wife, and Osborne Hall is my home. If you cannot respect that, you and I have nothing more to say to each other."

The tension in the room was suffocating, and the air was thick with unspoken challenges. Caroline, though tense, held her head high. No matter what happened, she would support Julian.

The marquess' gaze flicked between Julian and Caroline before he scoffed. "A true man does not squander what he's been given out of misplaced sentiment. You are a disappointment, Julian."

Julian took a deliberate step closer, his voice low and steady. "And you, Father, are a tyrant who confuses control with respect. But you won't control me any longer. I want the deeds in my hands today."

"You insolent—" The marquess stepped forward, his fists clenched, but Julian didn't flinch.

"Enough," Julian said firmly. His tone was so final and authoritative that even the marquess hesitated. "Mr. Harrington, please join us."

The marquess' mouth opened in shock as the door to the drawing room opened. A man in his early sixties entered, his bearing professional and unflappable, a leather satchel clutched in his hand.

"Good afternoon, my lord," Mr. Harrington said with a polite bow to the marquess before turning to Julian. "As requested, I have brought the necessary documents."

Caroline's eyes widened in surprise, and she turned her admiring glance to Julian. He'd planned this. He'd come prepared, anticipating his father's machinations.

The marquess' expression twisted in fury. "You've brought your lawyer into my house? Without my permission?"

Julian's voice was calm, but the steel beneath it was unmistakable. "It's not your house, Father. This is Thornfield House, the family seat. According to Grandfather's will, Osborne Hall was to belong to me. Or have you been lying about that, too?"

"How dare you—" The Marquess trembled with rage, but Julian cut him off.

"This ends today. If you value the legacy you claim to protect, you'll hand over the deeds now. Or we'll take this to court, with every detail of your manipulations laid bare."

Caroline held her breath. The Marquess looked ready to explode, his face red and his hands trembling with fury.

Finally, after what felt like minutes had passed, he let out a derisive snort. "Fine. Harrington, do what he asks. I've no time for these theatrics."

Julian didn't react outwardly, but Caroline felt his tension ease slightly as the lawyer moved forward. Papers were produced, signatures exchanged, and the deed to Osborne Hall stamped with the Thornfield and Osborne seals.

"Take your precious deed and get out." With one final glare, the marquess stormed from the room, his footsteps echoing down the hall.

Julian turned to Caroline, his expression softening as he reached for her hand. "It's done. Osborne Hall is ours, and no one—not even my father—will take it from us."

Tears pricked at Caroline's eye, but she smiled. "You've fought for us, Julian. For this life, we're building together. I'm so proud of you."

He brought her hand to his lips, pressing a lingering kiss to her knuckles. "I'll fight for you every day, Caroline. Whatever comes, we'll face it together."

She leaned into him, her heart full. Despite the storm they had just weathered, a new dawn was breaking—one they would share.

Epilogue

The sound of the horses' hooves on the packed dirt road was steady and rhythmic. The comfortable barouche swayed gently as it rolled along the country lane. Julian sat back, his cane leaning against his thigh, his eyes fixed on the woman across from him—Caroline, his wife.

The thought sent a rush of warmth through him. Her arms were crossed, her lower lip adorably pushed out in a pout as she stared to the side, avoiding his gaze.

"Are you going to tell me where we're going, Julian?" Caroline lifted her chin, her tone a mixture of curiosity and feigned irritation.

He smirked, unable to resist the urge to tease her. "Patience, my love. All will be revealed soon."

She turned sharply, fixing him with a glare that lacked malice. The corners of her mouth twitched, betraying her amusement. "You've been secretive about this 'outing' as you've labelled it. Four weeks at Osborne Hall, every day working together on the estate and the school, and you whisk me away without so much as a hint. It's positively cruel."

"Cruel?" Julian arched his brow, his lips curved into a slow smile. "You wound me. I thought you enjoyed surprises."

"Maybe." She shrugged and glanced at the hedgerows bordering the road; their leaves dappled in sunlight. "But I like to prepare for them."

He laughed. "You realise that if you prepare for it, it's no longer a surprise."

She glanced at him, her brow high. "I think I'll read."

"I assure you, no preparation is required for this surprise."

His gaze softened as he studied her. The sunlight caught in her curls, giving them a golden sheen, and her cheeks glowed with the health and happiness of the past weeks. She had taken to Osborne Hall with remarkable grace, her strength and warmth breathing new life into the estate and him.

He hadn't stopped thinking about this trip since the idea first came to him. Wrenwood Lodge was one of the most private places he could imagine—far from the responsibilities of Osborne Hall, far from the prying eyes of the ton. It was where they could simply *be,* allowing their intimacy to deepen without interruption.

Caroline shifted in her seat, her gaze flicking to him before darting away again. "You're enjoying this far too much."

"I'm enjoying the company." He curved his lips into a slow smile. "And watching you squirm."

She sighed dramatically. "Fine. I shall sit here silent and patient, like a good viscountess."

"Silent, perhaps," he teased. "Patient? I have my doubts."

Her laugh rang out, light and free, and Julian's chest tightened. How had he lived so long without this sound, without this woman who had brought such light into his life? Reaching across the space between them, he took her hand and kissed her knuckles, savouring how her cheeks pinked at the gesture.

"We're almost there," he promised softly. "Trust me, you'll love it."

The carriage crested a gentle hill, and the road opened into a view that took even Julian's breath away. Nestled in a small valley, surrounded by a forest of ancient oaks, the lodge came into view. The stone building was quaint and picturesque, with a thatched roof and ivy trailing up its walls. Smoke curled lazily from the two chimneys, and the front garden was awash with spring blooms—lavender, roses, and clusters of daisies that danced in the soft breeze.

Caroline gasped, sitting forward as her eyes widened. "Julian..."

He smiled, his chest swelling with pride. "Wrenwood Lodge. It's been in the Osborne family for generations. It's yours now, too, my love."

"Mine?" She turned to him, her expression full of wonder.

"Ours." He stepped from the carriage as it came to a halt and offered her his hand. "A place where we can escape the world, just the two of us."

She allowed him to help her down and swivelled to take in the scenery, her cheeks flushed with pleasure, and her lips parted in a delighted smile. "It's enchanting."

I hoped you'd think so." Julian tucked her arm into his, leading her toward the garden. "Shall we explore?"

"Yes, but only if you tell me everything about it." She laughed, her voice brimming with excitement.

He chuckled at her unbridled enthusiasm. "The lodge was built in 1670, originally as a hunting retreat. My ancestor won it in a rather scandalous card game. It's quiet, private, and some might say quite romantic."

"You planned this, didn't you? You knew exactly how romantic this would be." Caroline swatted his arm playfully. "If you expect me to cook, we will spend our time here eating bread and jam."

He nudged her. "Guilty as charged. I wouldn't mind eating bread and jam if I could be alone with you. But don't worry, I've spared you from cooking. The undercook, Nell and Finch, are already here to look after us. All we need to do is enjoy each other and the breathtaking view of sunrise filtering through the trees through the bedroom window."

Her blush deepened, and Julian's pulse quickened. He would never tire of seeing that soft colour rise in her cheeks.

They strolled through the garden, pausing by the brook that wound through the property. The sunlight danced on the water's surface, creating ripples of light that mirrored the way Caroline's laughter seemed to ripple through him.

"It's perfect." She let out a soft sigh.

Julian's gaze lingered on her profile, the way the sunlight caught in her hair and the peaceful smile that curved her lips. "As perfect as you."

She turned to him, her eyes warm and filled with affection. "It's perfect for us."

The moment stretched between them, the gentle rustle of leaves and the babbling of the brook the only sounds. The ache in his leg faded into the background, eclipsed by his sheer contentment with being here with her.

When they returned to the cottage, the sun began its descent, casting the valley in hues of gold and amber. A fire crackled warmly in the hearth, and the dining table was set for two with a simple but elegant meal.

Caroline stepped inside and turned in a slow circle. "It's even lovelier inside than I imagined."

Julian stepped behind her, resting his hands lightly on her shoulders. "I thought we could use some time away from the demands of Osborne Hall. Just you and me."

She turned to face him, her eyes shining with unshed tears. "A few days away just to relax and be together sounds like heaven."

He brushed a strand of hair from her cheek. "You deserve this and so much more."

"Oh, Julian." She stepped into his arms and rested her head against his chest. "I do love you so."

Julian tilted her chin upward, his lips brushing against hers in a slow and lingering kiss, a promise of all the moments yet to come.

"I love you, Caroline. More than I ever thought possible."

She traced the line of his jaw with her fingertips. "You deserve to be rewarded for your thoughtfulness."

Her smile transformed her entire countenance, radiating an armour-piercing warmth. The feather-light touch of her fingertips sent shivers coursing through his body, each caress igniting something primal deep within.

Julian tilted his head to her touch, a slow grin spreading across his face. His pulse quickened with anticipation. "Rewarded, you say?" The words emerged husky and laden with desire.

Her only response was to lift her skirts slightly and dart up the stairs, her laughter trailing behind her.

"Dinner can wait." He strode after her; the hunt he had discovered, was nearly as intoxicating as the capture.

In the master bedroom, Caroline's Spencer jacket was on the floor, her gown was tossed over a chair, and she wrestled with her undergarments. Her usual composure was replaced by endearing impatience.

He lit the wall sconces. She was too lovely to make love with in the dark, and a laugh rumbled from his chest at her eagerness. "Here, let me help with your stays. Where is Nell?"

"I told all the servants to stay in their accommodations tonight." The gleam in her gaze spoke volumes.

"Is that right?" Understanding dawned, sending a fresh wave of desire coursing through him. The little minx had orchestrated this evening of intimacy. A rush of affection for his passionate wife was quickly replaced by raw, consuming lust.

When she finally stood naked before him, Julian's breath caught. The transformation in her still amazed him. How quickly his once shy bride had bloomed into this confident temptress within the sanctuary of their bedroom. He held her at arm's length, drinking in every perfect curve, every shadow, every inch of beloved skin.

"You can stop ogling me. You have on far too many clothes." She attacked his cravat with delicious determination.

The command in her voice sent heat pooling in his belly. His clothes and boots quickly joined hers in their growing collection on the floor.

She teasingly stroked his already engorged cock from base to tip. "It looks like you are ready for me," she whispered huskily.

More than ready, he scooped her into his arms and tossed her onto the bed.

She shrieked, laughed and bounced. But when he climbed onto the bed to claim her, she slipped from underneath him with the agility of a cat, her eyes dancing with mischief. "It's my turn."

"Is that right?"

She tilted her chin. "I suggest you lie on your back and make yourself comfortable."

Julian's heart thundered against his ribs. This was a side of Caroline he'd never tire of discovering—confident, playful, commanding. He settled back against the pillows, his breath shallow with anticipation. The flicker of candlelight played across her skin, highlighting the subtle curves and valleys of her form and casting her in a golden glow. She was transformed into something otherworldly—a goddess come to earth to claim her due worship.

Julian's fingers twitched with the desire to touch, to claim her nipples, but he forced himself to remain still.

"My obedient husband." Her voice carried a note of satisfaction that sent heat coursing through his veins. She knelt beside him on the bed, her hand resting on his chest, directly over his thundering heart.

The touch of her lips against his collarbone drew a sharp intake of breath. She took her time exploring him, caressing light kisses across his throat and down his chest. She traced her fingertips over the scar on his shoulder with a tenderness that made his throat tight with emotion.

When her exploration ventured lower, Julian's hands fisted in the sheets. The combination of her bold touches and innocent expressions of discovery nearly undid him. "My love, you're proving quite adept at torture."

She lifted her head. "Perhaps. I learned from the best."

Her words referenced countless nights when he'd drawn out her pleasure until she'd begged for release. Now, it seemed, she intended to return the favour.

The sight of her—uninhibited, confident, and entirely in control—filled him with pride so fierce it bordered on pain.

When she straddled his thighs, the last remnants of his control threatened to snap. She must have read the desperate need in his expression, for she leaned forward to capture his lips. "Patience," she whispered against his mouth.

The kiss began as a whisper. Caroline's lips brushed his with deliberate restraint. Julian remained still beneath her, even as every fibre of his being urged him to surge upward and claim her mouth with the fierce hunger that consumed him.

She threaded her fingers through his hair, her nails grazing his scalp in a way that drew a low sound from his throat—somewhere between a groan and a plea. The kiss deepened by degrees, each subtle shift an exquisite torment. When her tongue traced the seam of his lips, he parted them willingly, surrendering to her exploration.

Controlled exploration became a raw need. Caroline's careful restraint crumbled as Julian's hands slid up her back, mapping the familiar terrain of her spine. Her body melted against his chest, skin to skin, and the kiss became wild and desperate, teeth grazing lips, breaths mingling, hearts thundering in matched rhythm.

When she finally drew back, her lips were swollen, her eyes dark with desire.

"My love." His voice broke with emotion. "You undo me completely."

She pressed her forehead to his, their breaths mingling in the scant space between them. "As you undo me."

He gripped her hips, and this time, she allowed the touch. The silk of her skin beneath his palms was eternally intoxicating. "You're driving me mad."

She smiled that same radiant smile that had started this evening's passionate encounter and traced his bottom lip with her thumb. "Good." She laced the single word with promise. "That's precisely my intention."

Julian groaned, head falling back against the pillows. At this moment, he would gladly grant her anything she desired. And judging by the triumphant gleam in her eye, she knew it. His breath caught sharply when her kisses traced the cut of his hip with deliberate intent.

"Tell me what you want." Authority threaded through her tone despite its gentleness.

The question drew a low laugh from him—half amusement, half desperate need. "You know precisely what I want, you wicked temptress."

"Perhaps." The smile of a goddess played at the corners of her mouth. "But I want to hear you say it."

Julian's grip on her hips tightened fractionally. Even now, she demanded his complete surrender, not just of his body, but of his pride, his control, his very essence. And God help him, he would give it all gladly, laying his soul bare before her if that was what she desired.

"Suck my cock, my stunning goddess. Shatter me."

She didn't answer, but with a sensual smile, she straddled his legs and bent low to lick from his base to tip. When she took his cock into her mouth, Julian's world narrowed to the exquisite sensations of Caroline's caress, each touch a declaration of ownership.

She took him deep into her throat, gagged a little and ran her tongue around the rim. He could swim forever in her mouth. She fell into a natural rhythm with her lips and cheeks. He fell into sync, rocking his hips up and down until he saw stars.

"My love." His words carried the weight of everything he felt for her —devotion, desire, and a depth of trust he had never expected to find in marriage. "You own me completely."

www.ingramcontent.com/pod-product-compliance
Lightning Source LLC
Chambersburg PA
CBHW071830190726
48292CB00005B/1702